*A*s Zee walked across the upper-school campus, she felt like an alien who had just landed on an unfamiliar planet. Sure, the upper-school kids were different, but it never mattered before. After all, they were the Others. Only, now she was one of them.

As Zee looked around, though, she didn't feel like one of them at all. For starters, she wore her red hair in a short bob. Most of the other girls had long blond or brown hair. Every single strand was perfectly in place and exactly the same length as the one right next to it. *Sigh*. How was she going to fit in here?

Read all of the Mackenzie Blue books

Mackenzie Blue

By
Tina Wells

Illustrations by Michael Segawa

HARPER
An Imprint of HarperCollins Publishers

Library of Congress Cataloging-in-Publication Data
Wells, Tina.
 Mackenzie Blue / Tina Wells ; illustrations by Michael Segawa. — 1st ed.
 p. cm.
 Summary: At the beginning of seventh grade, Mackenzie is worried—her best friend has
moved to France, someone steals her diary, she alienates her two new friends, and it looks
like she has lost her chance to win the Teen Sing contest.
 ISBN 978-0-06-158310-0 (pbk.)
 [1. Schools—Fiction. 2. Singing—Fiction. 3. Interpersonal relations—Fiction.
4. Friendship—Fiction. 5. Diaries—Fiction.] I. Segawa, Michael, ill. II. Title.
PZ7.W46846Mac 2009   2008045064
[Fic]—dc22   CIP
                                                                                     AC

Typography by Sasha Illingworth
12 13 14 15 16   LP/BR   10 9 8 7 6 5 4 3 2 1
❖
First paperback edition, 2013

In memory of my grandparents,
Loretta Mae Waters & Felder Featherstone Moragne

For Zoey & Azairea Bronson

Mackenzie Blue
and Her Crew

Landon Ally Zee

Kathi

Jen

✳ ① ✳
First Day Blues

Hi, Diary,

Today I'm kind of blue. Not blue as in Mackenzie Blue, which I always am. (Ugh! I can't believe I just made that joke.) This kind of blue is so not even funny. Not even a little.

First, my BFF Ally moves ALL THE WAY to PARIS, which is incredibly great for her. Who wouldn't want to live in France? The French have the most fabulous food, très chic fashion, and THE CUTEST guys. (Oooo la la!) Mom says Ally's move could be good for me, too. I'm not sure.

A *ding!* from Mackenzie Blue Carmichael's computer interrupted her. She slipped her diary and pen off her lap and rushed over to her desk. Awesome! An IM from Ally!

 SPARKLEGRRL: R u there?

Zee typed quickly.

 E-ZEE: Yes. I was just thinking of u!

 SPARKLEGRRL: Help! I h8 school! ☹

 E-ZEE: What's wrong??!

 SPARKLEGRRL: Everything. I can't sleep. No 1 here wants 2 talk 2 me. Maybe it's because I have NO idea how 2 dress like a French person. Did u know they have a thing against sneakers here?

 E-ZEE: Making friends isn't easy, especially in a new country!

So true. Zee became great friends with Jasper Chapman after he moved to Brookdale from London, England, over the summer. Jasper told Zee he had been lonely before he met her at the pool. Even with Jasper, Zee still missed Ally. They had been best friends and had gone to Brookdale Academy's lower school since preschool. And Zee needed Ally more than ever now that she was a seventh grader in Brookdale Academy's upper school—in a different building with different teachers.

 E-ZEE: I m nervous about my 1st day of school 2.

 SPARKLEGRRL: Y?

 E-ZEE: What if I can't find my way around? What if I 4get my locker combo? What if my life ends bc all I have time 4 is homework?

 SPARKLEGRRL: I know how u feel. I got lost AND 4got my combo. No hw yet tho.

E-ZEE: Ugh! Being a 7th grader in Upper is like being a kindergartner in Lower. U r 1 of the little kids—except no 1 thinks u r cute.

 SPARKLEGRRL: At least you are not alone. Like me.

 E-ZEE: No, u r not. U have me. BFF!!!!

Zee looked at the clock on her computer.

 E-ZEE: OMG! G2G! Time for school!

 SPARKLEGRRL: OK. LYLAS.

Zee grabbed her diary and dropped it in the black book bag that she'd decorated with pink and yellow felt flower cutouts. *I'll finish writing in my diary on my way to school*, she decided. As she walked downstairs, she texted Jasper on her Sidekick, which she'd covered with a bright blue skin that had a big pink Z in the middle.

>Want 2 meet up outside b4 school?

she typed on the keypad. Zee was new to the upper school, but Jasper was new to Brookdale Academy. He didn't know his way around at all.

His response came back right away.

>Sure.
I'm leaving now.
C u soon.

As Zee's dad drove her to school, Zee began a list of what was good and bad about Ally's living in France.

Good

1. I get to visit my BFF in France!
   (My parents already promised!)

2. I'll get a sneak peek at the newest
   French fashions before they come to
   LA!!

3. She can teach me French, and we can
   talk "in code" when I don't want my
   parents to know what I'm saying.

Bad

1. I'm miserable without my BFF here.

2. Ally's in a completely different time zone. What if I need her when she's sleeping—or she needs me when I'm at school?

3. What if Ally finds a new best friend in France?

Unfortunately, thanks to that last "bad," I think Mom might be wrong. Ally's move is still AWFUL!! ☹

And then there's my other big problem. But in this case, not so big. That's what makes it a problem. You know how most girls my age start getting boobs? Well, my body has decided to put all its energy into adding freckles to my face instead.

I probably just got three more freckles while I was writing that.

Zee

Zee closed her diary, slid the clasp into the latch, and put it back in her book bag. Then she looked out the SUV window.

"Dad, you can just stop the car now!" she said a little louder and more panicked than she'd meant to.

"But we're still a block from school, Zee," her father said. "I can't just leave you here on your first day."

"But I *want* you to."

J.P. Carmichael's right eyebrow rose up on his forehead, the way it always did when he was suspicious. "Why?" he asked.

"I don't want you to go out of your way."

"It's no problem," Zee's father said. "In fact, it's easier for me to just turn around in the school's drop-off circle."

Zee let out a deep sigh. "Dad, *please* stop the car."

Mr. Carmichael slowed down and steered to the curb. "Come on, Zee. What's going on?" he asked.

"It's your car, Dad," Zee explained. "It's kind of embarrassing." Zee had hoped to get a ride in her older brother's sporty red subcompact, but as usual Adam had overslept and was still shoveling corn flakes into his mouth when she was ready to go.

"You're embarrassed to be seen in a brand-new SUV?" he asked. "Would you prefer an ancient clunker with duct tape holding on the bumper?"

"What kind of gas mileage does the clunker get?" Zee asked.

Mr. Carmichael put his hand on his daughter's arm. "This isn't about the car, sweetie. You're just nervous about school. Don't worry—it will practically be the same as last year."

"Well, last year it was still a green school. You know, save the planet and end global warming so that your children will actually be able to breathe without a gas mask when they get older?" She opened the door, slid out of her seat, and planted her orange Converse high-tops on the sidewalk.

Mr. Carmichael sighed and ran his hand over the passenger seat. "But it's soooo comfortable."

"Sorry, Dad. I have to protect the family's reputation," Zee told him.

"But I am family."

"Yeah. And you're *kind of* making the rest of us look bad." She shut the door and gave her father a smile.

Mr. Carmichael hit the button to lower the automatic window. "Have a great first day, honey," he said.

"Thanks, Dad," Zee said, turning toward the school.

She had taken only a couple of steps when she heard her father shout. "Hey, Mackenzie!" Zee's dad called her by her full name only when he was working hard to stay calm.

"Yes, Dad?" Zee said super-sweetly, spinning around and

preparing for whatever was coming. Her father's eyebrow was up again.

"I think maybe the school gave you the wrong size uniform," he said. "Your skirt seems a little short."

Zee didn't bother to look down. She knew the exact length of her skirt. In the lower school, they had worn white blouses under blue plaid jumpers that hung nearly to their knees, but now that Zee was in seventh grade, she got to mix and match school-issued skirts, shirts, and sweaters. Although the pieces would never be trendy, they were way better than what she had had to wear to school before. And Zee planned to make the uniform—and herself—stand out. That meant wearing her sneakers, cool patterned socks, colorful beaded necklaces, bracelets, and earrings that she'd made herself— and shortening her hem.

"My skirt's fine," Zee said. "It just can't be any higher than my fingertips." She held her arms by her sides to demonstrate.

Mr. Carmichael squinted. "I think you might be bending your elbows a little," he said doubtfully.

Sighing, Zee stood at attention and stretched her arms down as far as they would reach. "See, Dad? Nothing to worry about. Totally regulation length. Mom hemmed it herself."

"At ease, soldier." Zee's father blew her a kiss. "Company dismissed."

"See ya!" Zee shouted with a big wave. She stuck her earbuds in, turned up her iPod, and made her getaway down the block before he could think of something else.

As Zee walked across the upper-school campus, she felt like an alien who had just landed on an unfamiliar planet (in her gas-guzzling spaceship). Sure, the upper-school kids were different, but it never mattered before. After all, they were the Others. Only, now she was one of them.

As Zee looked around, though, she didn't feel like one of them at all. For starters, she wore her red hair in a short bob. Most of the other girls had long blond or brown hair. Every single strand was perfectly in place and exactly the same length as the one right next to it. *Sigh*. How was she going to fit in here?

Just as Zee was about to run screaming to the wig store to cover her head, she stopped herself. *Hell-o*, she said silently. *What am I thinking? My red hair is what makes me*

Zee. If she wanted to stand out in the crowd, her hair was a great way to do it.

Zee scanned the school grounds, looking for Jasper. He was nowhere to be seen, but Zee did spot another person she knew—Kathi Barney. Even though she was a seventh grader, Kathi was standing with a group of eighth-grade boys—which made sense since she was about four inches taller than most of the boys her age anyway. Zee had always suspected whoever invented the word *popular* was thinking of someone *exactly* like Kathi. Also, the word *pretty*. And *perfect*. Perfect skin. Perfect brown hair. Perfect clothes. Perfect student.

Still, Zee decided not to go over to say hello—because Kathi had one imperfection. A big one. Her personality. Actually she had two personalities when it came to Zee—a nice one and a mean one. And the nice one came out only when she needed something.

Kathi's best friend, Jen Calverez, was right next to her. Jen was smaller than Kathi, with thick, wavy black hair. Jen was usually nice, and Zee wanted to say hi, but Jen was too close to Kathi at that moment. She might as well have been surrounded by yellow tape with DANGER: KEEP OUT printed all over. Zee stayed away.

What do I do now? she wondered. Suddenly her

phone rang. Jasper's number lit up on the screen. Thank goodness!

"Where *are* you?" Jasper asked in his British accent. "I've been looking everywhere."

Zee spotted a couple of juniors kissing as if their lips had been Krazy Glued together. From where she was standing, it looked like surgery might be the only way to get them apart. "I'm definitely *not* in Kansas anymore."

"Huh?"

"Never mind," Zee told Jasper. "I'm by the main entrance—near the giant palm tree."

"Don't move," Jasper said. "I'll be there straightaway."

Great, Zee thought. There was only one thing worse than wandering around alone with no one to talk to—*standing* alone with no one to talk to. But she wasn't going to abandon Jasper.

Zee felt like the newest inductee into the Geek Hall of Fame, when suddenly a ninth-grade girl raced toward her. Zee remembered her from the lower school. Excellent! Someone she recognized who actually seemed excited to see her. Unfortunately Zee was spacing on the girl's name. Lucy? Linda? Lorna?

"Lana!" a voice behind Zee shouted.

That's it! Zee said to herself, delighted. She turned to

see who had helped her out. Another girl was also running toward Zee. That's when Zee realized they weren't running to *her* at all. And they hadn't noticed that they were going to make a Zee sandwich if someone didn't move.

Zee stepped backward—*bam!*—right into Landon Beck's path! As she fell on to the ground, everything inside her bag spilled out. *How could this be happening?* Zee thought.

Landon was *the* most amazing guy at Brookdale Academy. Zee had had a crush on Landon for forever. She'd secretly daydreamed about eating lunch and doing homework with him. And she'd super-secretly hoped that he might even be her first kiss one day. (Only Ally knew that.)

"Hey, sorry," Landon apologized. His long bangs moved back and forth over his right eye in an I-don't-have-to-work-too-hard-to-look-this-good way. "I didn't see you."

Zee wanted to say, *No way was it your fault. I'm the one who fell into you.* But Landon was hypnotizing Zee with his incredible blue eyes. All she could say was "Uhhh."

"Are you all right?" Landon asked, reaching out his hand to help Zee to her feet. Landon had spent the summer at surf camp. He was so tan next to her pale complexion.

Say something good. Please, Zee silently begged herself. But that wasn't going to happen. "Uhhh."

Then out of nowhere, another familiar voice cut in. "Zee,

you should watch where you're going," Kathi said, pasting on a phony smile. "Unless you bumped into Landon on purpose." Landon had been Kathi's boyfriend on and off last year. Zee wasn't sure if they were on—or off—now.

"Are you hurt?" Jen asked.

Before Zee could answer, Kathi said, "Whatev." Then she glared at Zee behind Landon's back and silently mouthed, "Back off!"

As if, Zee thought. She felt her face turn red and worried that her skin would soon match the color of her hair from all of the embarrassment.

Finally Jasper arrived. "What's going on?" he asked. His white shirt was tucked into his dark blue uniform pants. The knot at the top of his blue tie formed a nearly perfect triangle, and the shoulders of his jacket were so straight you could have shelved books on them. His eyes, circled by silver wire-rim glasses, looked at Zee, at Landon, at the ground—anywhere but at Jen and Kathi—since Zee was just about the only girl who didn't make him completely nervous.

"I'll tell you later," Zee said. Desperate to get away, she waved her hand in the air at Jasper, the friends' signal to start walking—fast.

"Wait!" Landon called to Zee. "You forgot your book bag."

"Thanks," Zee said, taking it. *Would she be able to escape with even a tiny bit of cool left?* She bent over and gathered the contents, quickly shoving everything in.

Then Zee grabbed Jasper's arm and started to drag him inside the school. "Let's get out of here."

"Zee!" Landon shouted.

"What now?" Zee moaned under her breath. "Do I have toilet paper on the bottom of my shoe?" She turned around.

Landon wore the biggest, dimpliest smile. He pointed his cell phone at Zee and said, "Say cheese." Zee gave him a huge grin and posed while he took a picture. "I'll email it to you."

Tugging Jasper's arm, Zee pulled him into the building.

"Hey!" Jasper protested. "You'll wrinkle my jacket."

"Sorry," she apologized, releasing her grip. "I just want to get out of here as fast as possible," she explained.

"What a daft way to start the year, huh?" Jasper said.

"Oh, it was okay." The *cutest* boy in school had a photo of *her* on his cell phone!

2

A Sour Note

"Good morning and welcome to Brookdale Academy Upper School," a cheerful woman said from the other side of a table covered with stacks of papers and boxes. "I'm Mrs. Sayles, the school secretary. And your name is . . . ?"

"Zee." Mrs. Sayles smiled expectantly as if she were looking at a toddler trying to say her first words. *Duh!* "Sorry. Mackenzie."

The secretary just stared and waited. After a pause, she finally asked, "And what is your first name?"

Zee snapped out of her

own trance, shaking her head. "That
is my first name."

"Okay. Mackenzie what?"

"Mackenzie Blue," she said matter-of-factly. Mrs. Sayles
began flipping through some cards in a file box.

"Carmichael," Jasper added. "Mackenzie Blue Carmichael."

"Thanks," Zee mouthed to her friend. She knew she had
been nervous about the upper school, but she hadn't realized *how* nervous. And falling down in front of everyone—
including Kathi—definitely hadn't helped.

Mrs. Sayles pulled out a couple of cards and handed the
first one to Zee. "Here's your class schedule."

Zee took the card and looked at it. Seven classes! How
did they squeeze seven classes into one measly day? Plus
lunch! Plus time in between classes! And what if every
teacher gave her homework *every day*?

Then Mrs. Sayles handed her the second card. "And here's
your locker assignment with your combination. Just follow
the instructions at the top—turn to the right until you get
to the first number, then turn to the left, passing the number
one time and stopping on it the second time around, then
turn to the right to the third number."

Mrs. Sayles smiled, and Zee tried to reboot her brain.

"Um . . . could you repeat that?" she asked.

"No need," Jasper cut in. "I'll show her." He spun Zee around. "Look at the queue." The line had grown behind them.

"Oops!"

Then Jasper reached out his right hand to shake Mrs. Sayles's. "I'm Jasper Chapman."

Zee couldn't believe what she was hearing! Jasper wasn't stammering or looking at the ground. He didn't sound nervous at all. Instead of being worried about information overload, he confidently pushed his glasses higher on his nose.

Mrs. Sayles smiled and handed Jasper his cards. "Welcome to Brookdale Academy." Zee relaxed, happy that Jasper was there for her.

Zee looked at her schedule. "Cool beans!" she shouted. "I have seventh-grade instrumental music first period." She loved music more than just about anything else. Over the summer, she'd spent a huge amount of time writing her first real song. Her diary was full of cross-outs and scribbles and revisions, but Zee was finally close to finishing it. Then she'd cut a demo, sign a record deal, and become a pop phenomenon. (So maybe it wouldn't be *quite* so easy, but Zee had no problem working hard for her dreams.)

"My schedule says I have music first period, too," Jasper said, smiling.

"Excellent! Let's go!" Zee started to walk faster.

"Hey!" Jasper called to her. "You're going too fast."

"I can't help it. This class is going to be so cool!" she said. "Mrs. Bradley is an amazing teacher. Brookdale's music program is practically famous. They win all kinds of awards—mostly because of her. The symphony orchestra goes everywhere. They've even performed in Europe." Zee and Jasper arrived at the classroom door. "Room 124. This is it." They stepped inside.

"No one's here," Jasper said, scanning the empty room.

"We can just hang out until Mrs. Bradley comes," Zee said, looking around. A big wooden teacher's desk sat directly in front of the middle of a whiteboard. Two rows of chairs, arranged in semicircles faced that, and a shiny black grand piano sat off to the side. Then Zee noticed a bright red flyer on the wall. "I don't believe it!" she shouted as she read the sign. "*Teen Sing* is going to hold auditions at Brookdale Academy!"

"What's *Teen Sing*?" Jasper asked.

"It's this amazing singing contest for twelve- to sixteen-year-olds. They have a bunch of local competitions all over the country. If you win one of those, you get to go to the national competition. And if you win that, you get a recording contract!" Zee was talking so fast, even she was having trouble keeping up. "You didn't have that in England?"

"Um . . . maybe," Jasper said, biting his lip. Zee laughed. *Teen Sing* could have been the hottest British phenomenon since the Spice Girls, but since it had nothing to do with soccer, Jasper wouldn't have noticed. He'd rather read a book than turn on the TV—unless a soccer game was on. But despite their differences, somehow Zee and Jasper clicked as friends. "Are you going to enter the *Teen Sing*-along?" Jasper wondered.

Zee pointed to the flyer. "*Teen Sing,*" she explained, wondering if it was actually too late to save Jasper. "There is *no* way I am *not* going to compete. It's going to be so awesome. Brookdale's auditorium is state of the art. It has the best equipment."

Zee paused and looked at Jasper. "Am I talking too much?" But before he could answer, she said, "I'm just excited. I really, really want to win."

"Win what?" a voice asked. Zee looked back and saw Kathi had entered the room with Jen.

"Nothing," Zee answered quickly before Jasper could. She did *not* want to hear Kathi's opinion on the topic.

Kathi looked around as if she were lost. "I must be in the wrong room," she said. "I thought this was instrumental music."

"It is," Zee told her.

"Then what are you doing here?"

"I play guitar."

"I know that," Kathi said. "I thought you had to play a *real* instrument to be in here. Guitar doesn't really count since you only have to learn, like, three chords."

"I hope it counts," a voice said from the hallway. A man wearing a white button-down shirt that was only partially tucked into his dark blue pants appeared in the doorway. In one hand, he carried a mug with coffee sloshing over the side. Little brown drops splashed on to the disorganized stack of papers he had braced against his chest with the other hand. "Guitar's my instrument—well, one of them."

"Are you a student?" Kathi asked. Zee thought he could be a student, too. He didn't look much older than her brother, Adam.

The man placed his coffee cup on the teacher's desk. "No, I'm Mr. Papademetriou."

Kathi stared at him blankly. "Mr. P," he continued. "The teacher."

"The *teacher*?" Kathi asked. "No way!"

As Zee watched his papers slide down next to his coffee mug, she could see what looked like a jelly stain right in the middle of his tie. She also noticed that he was wearing a pair of Converse sneakers just like hers, only his were black.

"Actually I'm the substitute," Mr. P continued. "Until they officially hire me."

"Why would they do that?" Kathi asked.

Mr. P's face fell, and Zee decided she had to rescue him from Kathi. "What happened to Mrs. Bradley?" she asked just as Landon and his best friend, Marcus Montgomery, entered the room. Even with their loose ties, untucked shirts, and baggy uniform pants, they looked more like teachers than the teacher.

Mr. P leaned away from the crowd of students standing in front of him. "Mrs. Bradley's husband was transferred to the East Coast for work."

"Forever?" Marcus asked. Zee was glad Marcus joined in. He was outgoing and friendly with everybody.

Mr. P nodded. "I'm the new music teacher."

"The *substitute*," Kathi quickly added.

"That's cool," Marcus said.

The first-period bell rang loudly overhead, startling the young teacher. Relief washed over his face, though, when he realized he could begin class. "Okay, everyone," Mr. P said, with a loud *clap*. "Please find a seat."

As the seventh graders scrambled for chairs, Zee smiled nervously at Jasper. This was *not* the teacher she had promised him and raved about—not even close. "Remain calm," she tried to telegraph to him mentally—although based on the way she felt inside, she was pretty sure it looked more like, "EVACUATE THE PREMISES IMMEDIATELY! EMERGENCY!"

Mr. P took roll. As he announced names, students responded, "Here." But when Mr. P called out, "Chloe

Lawrence-Johnson," no one answered. Zee figured it was a new girl since she didn't recognize the name. Mr. P repeated the name as everyone looked around. No response.

How could anyone miss the first day of school? Zee wondered. That was like missing Christmas. There were no do-overs for either one.

Zee and the others watched and waited to see what Mr. P would do after he finished reading off names. For a while he did nothing—unless strumming his fingers on the desk counted as something. Then he circled around to the front of the desk. Some teachers leaned against the front of theirs, but Mr. P *sat on* his.

"I guess I should tell you a little bit about myself," he said, looking from one face to the next. "I just got back to the United States after living all over Europe for a few years."

Cool beans! Zee was dying to go to Europe. The new teacher might be interesting after all.

"This is my first year teaching, but I've been a musician since I was about your age," he trailed off quietly. "Do you guys have any questions for me?" No one raised a hand. "Anyone?" he said, although Zee was sure he looked at Kathi in a way that said, *Except you. I don't want you to ask me a question.*

Zee racked her brain, then stuck her arm in the air. Mr. P pointed in her direction. "Yes?"

"Who's your favorite musician?" Zee asked.

"Bob Dylan," Mr. P answered immediately.

Kathi groaned.

"You don't like Dylan?" Mr. P asked her.

Before answering, Kathi rolled her eyes at Jen. But Zee could tell that Jen was only pretending to understand when Kathi heaved a dramatic sigh. "I just expected a more original answer from a music teacher," she said.

"Who's your favorite?" Mr. P asked.

"Anyone but Bob Dylan," Kathi said. "He's way overrated."

Mr. P was silent. Zee knew he was trying to figure out what to say next. Finally he spoke to the class. "I'd like everyone to write down a little bit about yourself—what instrument you play, how long you've played . . . " He paused to think some more. "Oh, and what you like best about music."

Everyone took out a piece of paper and began writing— including Zee.

Name: Mackenzie Blue Carmichael
Instrument: Guitar
Number of years: 3

What I Like Best About Music

1. You can say what you're feeling
   without using words.
2. You can sing while you're doing just
   about everything else. Except sleeping.
   Unless you ~~talk~~ sing in your sleep.
3. It's a great way to become famous if
   you don't like sports.
4. It makes me happy.
5. It makes me Zee!

As Zee finished, Kathi walked to the front of the room and handed Mr. P her piece of paper. She had covered the entire sheet with information about herself.

"Thanks," Mr. P said, taking the assignment.

"No prob," Kathi told him, heading back to her seat. "I'm surprised you didn't ask us to write about what we did over our summer vacation," she mumbled to no one in particular.

One by one, the other students finished and gave Mr. P their papers. As Zee delivered hers, the bell rang overhead. The first period—or in Kathi's case, the first round—was over.

3

The New Girl

*Z*ee grabbed her book bag and turned to Jasper. "Let's go!" she said as she hurried past the other students toward the door. As much as Zee liked music, she couldn't wait to get out of the room. After only one class period with Kathi, she'd had enough of her to last a week. Mr. P seemed nice but nervous. She hoped he got over it fast.

Just as Zee took a step into the hall—CRASH!—she slammed into another body. The two of them bounced off each other in different directions, and the girl barely missed ricocheting off a senior boy who could have been a body double for a gorilla.

"Ohmylanta!" Zee declared. How could this be happening again?

The girl looked at Zee. "What did you say?" Her dark hair was pulled back in a long ponytail, which made her green eyes stand out.

Zee shrugged. "Oh, it's nothing. It's just something I say when I get nervous or surprised!"

The girl laughed. "That's funny! I'm from Atlanta, Georgia. I thought maybe you knew that." Zee had never seen the girl before, but her Southern accent definitely told Zee she was *not* from Brookdale. As if the girl could read Zee's mind, she said, "But that would be totally weird since you don't know me." She paused. "I'm Chloe. I'm sorry I ran into you."

"It was *so* not your fault," Zee said. "I think aliens abducted me last night and turned me into a human-size piece of metal. It turns out the rest of the world are magnets."

"Maybe you just have a magnetic personality!" Chloe suggested with a smile. "Did the aliens name you?"

Zee nodded. "Mackenzie. You can call me Zee. Everyone does—except teachers. And sometimes my parents. And their friends."

"Wow! That's a lot of information."

"Too much?" Zee asked.

"A teeny bit." Chloe laughed. "You're not the only one having a bad day. It took me forever to get my schedule figured out, and *then* I went to the wrong classroom. I sat in photography for fifteen minutes before I figured out my mistake. Now I have to find *another* class."

"What class did you miss?" asked Zee.

"Music," Chloe replied.

"Oh, I was in that class! You're Chloe Lawrence-Johnson! What do you have second period?" Zee asked.

Chloe looked at her schedule. "English."

"Me, too. Let's look for it together."

"Maybe we'll find it twice as fast," Chloe said.

Zee rolled her eyes. "Or get twice as lost." The girls started walking.

Behind her, Zee heard someone clear his throat. She looked up. Oops! Jasper. "Sorry," Zee said. Sometimes he was soooo quiet—especially around girls—that it was easy to forget he was even there.

Zee introduced her two newest friends to each other. "Hi," Jasper said quickly. "Maths class is in the other direction. I'll meet up with you at lunch." He started to walk away, then added, "Try not to forget about me—please."

"I won't!" Zee promised.

The girls began to search for their English room. "I like

your bag," Zee told Chloe as they wove in and out of the other students. The body was a diamond pattern with black, green, and red squares. "Where did you get it?"

"I made it."

"You made it? Cool beans!"

"I couldn't find anything I liked in the store. I wish I'd seen yours."

Zee laughed. "I didn't buy it like this," she said. "It was plain, so I decorated it."

"Oh, *my* gosh! It looks better than the ones in the boutiques in Los Angeles. Can I look at it?"

Zee slipped it off her shoulder. "If I can see yours?"

The girls swapped bags. Zee couldn't believe how great Chloe's looked. "This would cost over two hundred dollars in a store."

Chloe looked down at herself. "Next I'm gonna try to do something about this uniform." She tugged on her pants and stuck out her tongue. "Blech. I hope I can make it look as awesome as you did."

"Really?" Zee could feel herself blushing from the compliment. She couldn't believe that on the very first day of school she'd found another friend—one who liked to individualize her stuff as much as Zee did!

The rest of the morning went by in a flash. Every teacher explained the rules that *must* be followed, handed out forms that *must* come back the next day, and gave each student textbooks that *must* have weighed a ton. It helped that Chloe had been in all of Zee's classes. But her new friend wasn't taking her next class with her—French. Zee didn't know any other seventh graders who were.

When Zee found out Ally was moving to France, she had signed up for French right away. She wanted to visit her friend, and when she did, she wanted to be able to read and speak well enough to avoid total embarrassment. Like accidentally ordering frog legs instead of ice cream. Or asking for the kitchen instead of the bathroom.

Thinking about it made Zee miss Ally more than ever. She pulled out her Sidekick and stared at it. Because it was too expensive, she wasn't allowed to text or call her best friend without permission. *But I need to talk to* someone, Zee thought. Then she remembered someone who might be even lonelier than she was.

Zee tapped out a message to Jasper.

>K?

Jasper wrote back,

>Brilliant!
My maths teacher sez my accent is charming.
G2G.

Zee giggled as she turned the corner of the foreign language hall. Jasper may have been a brand-new student, but he was already fitting in.

When Zee got to the French room, she discovered she wasn't alone. Jen was already there. "Hey, Zee!" she shouted, motioning for Zee to sit next to her. Ugh! If Jen was there, it wouldn't be long before Kathi was, too.

"Don't you want Kathi to sit there?" Zee asked.

"She's taking Spanish."

"Then why aren't *you*?"

"Mamá y Papá me están haciendo tomar francés," Jen explained. Even though Zee didn't grow up speaking Spanish like Jen, she had studied it since kindergarten, so she knew Jen's parents were making her take French.

"I guess it's *adios*, easy class, for you," Zee said.

"*Bonjour!*" Marcus greeted the girls as he slid backward into the chair in front of Jen. "Just the people I want to see."

"Why?" Jen asked, leaning forward.

"Look for a text message from me later today. I'm having a party."

"A party? What's the excuse this time?" Jen asked, grinning. Set against her dark hair, Jen's smile was incredibly bright.

Marcus looked up at the ceiling as if he were deep in thought. "Beginning of the school year. End of summer. Finally making it to the upper school. First day of the rest of your life," he rattled off. "Take your pick." Marcus had so many parties, he never needed an excuse. They were always amazing. He usually had a DJ—sometimes even a live band.

"I'll take first-day-of-the-rest-of-your-life party," Jen said, giggling.

"I'm definitely going to the finally-making-it-to-the-upper-school party," Zee said, laughing.

Who knew Jen could be so fun—and funny? It was just another bit of first-day-of-school weirdness. But this time it was a *good* thing.

4
(Not So) Hot Lunch

Zee zigzagged through the cafeteria crowd, clutching her lunch tray so hard her knuckles ached. The lentil loaf was so soggy it almost looked like stew. She figured she would just survive on the organic apple until she got home. Each time another student whizzed past, Zee's plate slid close to the edge. Somehow her bottle of water slid the opposite direction. Just as she got everything in place, it happened again.

What had Zee been thinking? She had decided that buying hot lunch on the first day would make her feel more like a mature upper schooler. Bad idea. She felt more like a kindergartner who'd wandered into the wrong lunchroom.

It didn't help that she was still carrying around her book

bag, now completely loaded with the textbooks she'd collected that morning.

It wasn't as though Zee had never felt out of place before, but usually Ally was there—and feeling just as out of place. Together they had always managed to figure everything out. Now Zee resembled the main character in an Animal Planet special. *Without the other members of her group to guide her, the young chimp looks for a safe place to eat her lunch. Will she find it? Or will she be eaten first?*

Zee took a deep breath and scanned the room, trying to find a friendly face.

"Hi, Zee."

"Aaaaaa!" Zee jumped, her plate taking a dive off the side of her tray. Her brother, Adam, who had snuck up behind her, grabbed it before it hit the ground. "Adam! You scared me!" Zee cried, chasing after her water bottle. "Were you sent by the chimp leader?" she asked when she returned to where Adam was standing.

"Huh?"

"Never mind."

"Actually I came over to save you, so you don't sit in the wrong place and end up with your underwear flying from the flagpole, but if you don't want my help . . . ," he said, then turned to walk away.

"No! Wait!" Zee called out a little too loudly. When Adam turned around, she said in a normal voice, "What do I need to know?"

Adam pointed across the noisy room to an area all the way over to the farthest corner. "Those are the seventh-grade tables over there."

"I thought there was no assigned seating," Zee said.

"The administration doesn't assign—the seniors do." Great. Another reminder that Zee was on the bottom rung of the upper-school ladder. She glared at her brother.

Adam held his hands in the air. "Don't blame me. I'd let you sit at a better table, but this is the social order."

"Just what I thought—the seniors *are* like chimps," Zee said.

"You're weird," Adam said. Then he pointed at the senior table. "Just don't make the mistake of sitting there—like that girl."

Oh no! *That girl* was Chloe, eating at the end of the forbidden table. Zee rushed over to get her. "Let's sit over here," she said, swooping in to save her new friend. As the girls switched tables, Zee realized her work wasn't done. Jasper was reading a book at the eighth-grade table.

She tapped Jasper on the shoulder. "Want to sit with us?"

Jasper had just bitten into his apple. "Pffwmph," he said as he stood.

As the three of them finally made it over to the right place, Marcus waved and motioned for them to sit across from him. Excellent! Marcus was next to Landon. Zee could sit close to her crush without even trying.

Of course, Kathi was on the other side of Landon, and as Zee got closer, she could hear her talking to Jen. "I mean, I know lots of upperclassmen, but I would never sit at their tables—unless they invited me, which they eventually will." She laughed. "But *not* the first day."

Zee dropped her tray on the table. "I think they should just be honest and start calling it *lukewarm* lunch from now on," she said to let Kathi know they could hear her talking about them.

Unfortunately for Kathi she had failed to make Chloe feel bad about sitting at the wrong table. "Hi, y'all," Chloe said cheerfully. "I'm new here—in case you couldn't tell." Then she looked right at Kathi. "You sound like you know what you're doing. If I have any problems, I'll come right to you!"

Kathi looked like someone had just told her she had a giant piece of spinach on her front tooth.

"Hi, I'm Marcus." Behind his black glasses, his eyes lit up as he spoke. "I'm having a welcome-to-Brookdale party. I'll text you the information if you give me your cell phone number."

"I have to check," Chloe said. "I just got a phone, and I don't know the number yet."

Kathi made a miraculous recovery from her stunned condition. "You *just* got a cell phone?" she exclaimed. "Where'd you move from? The last century?"

"Not hardly," Chloe said with a friendly smile. "Atlanta, Georgia."

Marcus unwrapped his sandwich, then held half up to Chloe. "Want some?" he asked. "It's tuna fish."

"No, thanks," Chloe said. "I'm a vegetarian."

Kathi forced an incredibly loud laugh, then looked around as if she expected everyone to join her. Of course, Jen followed her lead, but no one else did.

"What's up with that?" Kathi asked.

"I don't eat meat."

"I know that. Why not?"

Chloe shrugged. "I guess 'cause I just don't want to."

Zee thought Kathi's head might explode when Landon said, "Cool. I've been thinking about becoming a vegetarian, too."

Kathi shook her head so furiously you could hear her earrings jingle. "Oh, you don't want to do that," she told him. The fury in Kathi's eyes looked like it would burn a hole through

Chloe. "It'll make you look small . . . and kind of . . . sick."

"Well, I've always looked this way," Chloe said. "But I just became a vegetarian last year. And I love animals, so it was sort of natural for me."

"What*ev*," Kathi said, defeated.

Whoa. This girl knew exactly how to get to Kathi.

For the rest of lunch, Kathi was quiet. She practically didn't speak again until the other seventh graders began comparing schedules. Zee, Jasper, Chloe, Landon, Marcus, Jen, and Kathi all had seventh-grade science—Introduction to the Environment—together right after lunch.

"I'm sure we're going to get another fat book for that class,"

Zee said. She lifted her heavy bag onto her shoulder. "I guess I should make some room in here. I gotta go to my locker."

"I'll go with you," Chloe volunteered.

Jasper looked from Kathi to Jen, then stood up. "Me, too," he said. Zee guessed Marcus and Landon weren't enough protection against the girls for Jasper.

As the three of them crossed the noisy cafeteria, Zee dropped her water bottle in the plastic recycling bin. Then she waved to Adam, who smiled back.

"Is that your boyfriend?" Chloe asked.

Shocked, Zee stumbled. "No way," she said. "He's my brother."

"Oh," Chloe said, biting her lower lip and glancing back at Adam.

Zee entered the science room and glanced around. It didn't look like any of her other classrooms. Instead of separate desks arranged in rows, high tables were spaced evenly throughout the room. Each one had a sink in the middle and two tall chairs behind it.

Ms. Merriweather, the science teacher, looked up and smiled. "Welcome. Just take a seat anywhere." Zee grabbed the closest chair, and Jasper climbed into the chair next to her as Chloe sat on the other side.

About halfway into the period, Ms. Merriweather began matching lab partners. Because her life was perfect, Kathi was with Landon. Zee and Jen were together. Zee wasn't thrilled, but since Jen had actually been nice to her in French class, she figured it would be okay.

Ms. Merriweather paired Chloe with Jasper. Zee was happy that they didn't have to sit with kids they didn't know.

Then their teacher began explaining the big project every set of lab partners would do. "Brookdale Academy is a LEED-certified school," she began. "LEED stands for Leadership in Energy and Environmental Design. Here at Brookdale, we find ways to conserve energy and water and to make less of an impact on our natural environment."

If your dad drives an SUV, I hope you don't have to work extra hard to make up for it, Zee thought.

"Throughout the year, we'll be studying environmental issues," Ms. Merriweather went on. "Each month, one set of lab partners will present a project that explores how this school can do even more to take care of the planet." She put a sheet of paper on the lab table closest to her and told everyone to sign up for the month in which they wanted to present their project. The first set of partners chose June, and the next picked May.

Jen and Zee sat at the third table, and like the students before her, Jen wanted to put off the project as long as possible. "Let's sign up for April," she suggested. Zee was psyched to do the project in April. Earth Day was in April, and she knew they could plan something really awesome.

Jasper and Chloe were the last partners to sign up, so they got October. They had to present the first project. But they didn't seem to mind. They had their heads together and were talking a mile a minute.

Jen sighed. It looked as though it took all the energy she had to prop her head up with the palm of her hand. "Why do we have to come up with ideas for the school? Isn't that the teachers' job?"

"I think it's cool that the students have a say," Zee answered.

"What if we don't want to?"

A pang of jealousy shot through Zee as she turned around again. Jasper and Chloe were busy sharing ideas about their science project.

After school, Zee hopped out of Adam's car and tore through the front door. "Hi, Mom!" she shouted.

"I'm in the TV room," Ginny Carmichael called back.

Zee took a quick detour to greet her mother, dropped her book bag on the couch, and shot upstairs to email Ally. When she turned on her computer, she saw her best friend had already written. Yay!

Zee,
Guess what?!!? When I complained to Mom and Dad about not fitting in at school, they signed me up for French tutoring. Great—NOT. I hate being the new student!!! (In case you can't tell.) ARFN (Au Revoir For Now).
BFF (LYLAS),
A

Boo! Zee quickly typed a reply.

Hey!
I know how you feel!!! Upper School is a new
language. My survival depends on becoming fluent!!!

<u>Zee's Report Card</u>

Subject: Landon
Grade: B-
Comments: He's cuter than ever, but I totally
embarrassed myself in front of him.

Subject: Kathi
Grade: F
Comments: She still wants to make everyone else
miserable—even the teachers.

Subject: Friends
Grade: A+
Comments: There's a new girl named Chloe. And
she and Jasper get along. I can't wait for you to
come and meet them. They're really cool.

BFF—Z

5

Missing!

As soon as Zee hit Send, her Sidekick rang. A text message from Jasper.

>Can I borrow An Inconvenient Truth?

Zee sent back a message.

>Book or DVD?

>Book.

>Sure. Y?

>Science project.

Zee laughed. Jasper was the only person she knew who would give himself homework on the first day of school.

Thirty minutes later, Jasper rang the doorbell.

"You forgot to put on a tie," Zee said after she opened the door. Jasper had changed into a pair of khaki chinos with a navy blue polo shirt. Zee was certain it was the uniform for the Sprigg School, another private school in Brookdale.

"I hope you amuse yourself," Jasper said, stepping into the foyer.

"I do."

Zee's mother placed a giant flower arrangement on to a table by the door. "Hello, Jasper," Mrs. Carmichael said as she adjusted the stems. "Would you like a snack?" Ally always called her Brookdale's Snack Queen. No one ever went hungry at Zee's.

"Yes, please," Jasper said eagerly. "I am a bit peckish. If you don't mind."

"You're always so polite." Mrs. Carmichael turned to Zee. "Why don't you two wait in the TV room, and I'll bring it in to you."

Zee shoved her book bag off the couch, dropped herself

on to the cushion, and picked up a Wii game control. "Wanna play?" she asked.

"Of course," Jasper said, picking up another remote and sitting next to Zee.

"Big Brain Academy or Boogie?"

Jasper gave her a sideways look. "Big Brain Academy."

"You just can't get enough school, can you?"

"I *can* get enough dancing," Jasper said. "Now prepare for me to crush you with my enormous brain."

After a while, Mrs. Carmichael entered the room with a tray overloaded with pita chips, cheese, beans, and salsa. At the

sight of the feast, Jasper forgot all about the video game and nearly dived on to the tray. "Thank you, Mrs. Carmichael!"

"*Bon appetit,*" Mrs. Carmichael said as she turned to leave the room. Given Zee's mother's hostess obsession, that was one French phrase she already knew.

Zee watched Jasper as he scooped chips into his mouth, barely taking time to breathe. So much for "proper" English manners. "I'll leave you guys alone and go get that book," she said, grabbing a gooey lump for herself.

"*Mmmphssst,*" Jasper replied as he took a swig of lemonade.

When Zee returned, Jasper was licking his fingers. "Did you get enough to eat?" she asked sarcastically, handing him the book.

"I have a healthy appetite," he defended himself.

"Sometimes I think you're just using me for my snacks," Zee said.

"Oh! That's a *brilliant* idea." Jasper looked at his watch. "I'd better go. I need to get started on my project." He picked up the tray and carried it into the kitchen. "Thanks again, Mrs. Carmichael. That was delicious."

"You're welcome, Jasper," she said. As he walked away, Zee heard her mother mumble, "What a nice boy." Zee rolled her eyes.

That night, Zee laid out her clean uniform alongside a pair of multicolored striped tights. To top it off, she chose a necklace with a peace sign pendant that she'd made out of sparkly red beads. Then she put on her polka dot pajamas, pulled up her comforter, and sank into her pillow.

"Ohmylanta!" Zee sprang out of bed like a bird out of a cuckoo clock. *I almost went to sleep on the first day of school without writing in my diary.* She already had an idea for a list—"Ten Reasons It's Going to Be an Awesome Year After All."

Zee reached into her book bag. There were pencils and pens, her new binder, and a couple of spiral notebooks. But no diary. Zee looked again. She took everything out, one by

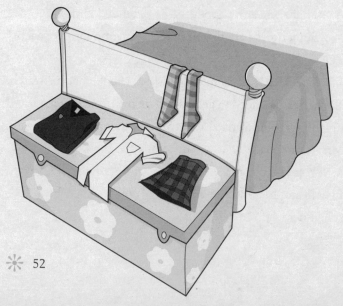

one. Still no diary. She looked in every compartment of her binder. Nothing. She put all the items back in her bag. Then she did it all again.

The diary was gone!

"Double ohmylanta!" Zee shouted. But just as she was about to panic, her memory flashed. *It probably fell under the couch when Jasper and I were playing video games*, she told herself. She ran downstairs, got on her hands and knees, and searched the floor. A pen. A quarter. Three pennies. No diary. She pulled off the cushions. She looked in vases and on bookcases, underneath the rug, and behind throw pillows. She raced up to her room and searched in every imaginable space. She even checked inside the refrigerator.

Adam looked up from the kitchen table, where he was working on his MacBook. "What are you looking for?" he asked.

"My diary," Zee told him.

"I ate it," he said, then continued typing.

"Ha ha," Zee said, eyeing her brother suspiciously. "You

wouldn't know anything about why it's missing, would you?"

"Hmmm. Stealing your diary? Well, that would be lots of fun, but right now I've got more important things to do—like work on these college applications," he said. "Now quit bothering me." Zee knew Adam was telling the truth. He'd been obsessing over college applications for weeks. Princeton and Berkeley were his top picks.

Zee had been only two places that day—her house and school. Oh no! If the diary was at school, maybe someone had found it and read it. Zee imagined the next day's morning announcements:

> "Attention, students! Today's lunch is chicken salad and green beans. Mackenzie Blue Carmichael sometimes dreams that she shows up for school wearing only her underwear. Also, she has been crushing on Landon for years. Please stand for the Pledge of Allegiance."

The thought of public humiliation was unbearable. Zee *had* to find her diary. She went back to the TV room and searched again.

"What's going on?" Mrs. Carmichael asked as a flying couch cushion nailed her in the face.

"Sorry, Mom," Zee said, then quickly added, "I can't find my diary."

"When did you see it last?" her mom asked, concerned. That was one of the great things about Zee's mom. She understood that a missing diary was a real crisis.

Zee thought. "On my way to school."

"I bet it's in Dad's car."

Of course! Maybe she had accidentally left it on the seat.

Mr. Carmichael stepped into the room and surveyed the mess. "Should we call the police? They'll want to catch whoever did this before he hits another house."

"I need to look in your car for my diary, Dad," Zee explained. "Can I have your keys?"

Mr. Carmichael's eyes grew wide. "Ummm . . . I'll help you look, sweetie," he offered. Zee knew he only wanted to save his car from the same fate as the TV room. But she didn't care if he searched, too, since she could use the help.

Zee and her dad looked under the seats, in the glove box, and even where the spare tire was stored, but they couldn't find the diary. After having torn up both the house and the car, Zee had to admit, the diary wasn't at home.

That night, Zee had trouble sleeping. Her mind raced. When had she lost the diary? Before school? Lunchtime?

Was it in her book bag when she'd gotten home? It was no use. She just couldn't remember.

Zee climbed out of bed and reached for a notebook. On a piece of paper, she scribbled a new heading for her list:

Top Ten Most Embarrassing
Confessions in My Diary
or
Why I Should Consider
Being Homeschooled

The Message

 E-ZEE: R u there?

Zee IM'ed Ally the next morning.

 SPARKLEGRRL is offline

She's probably in school, Zee decided. Would she ever get used to the new schedule?

Zee pulled a piece of paper out of her printer.

Hi, ~~Diary~~ Piece of Paper,

   I didn't think it was possible for me to miss Ally more than I did yesterday. Or the day before. Guess what? It is. Best friends and crises go together. But we're so far apart. And I have <u>no</u> idea how to get through this without her.

Zee

Zee stared at the nothingness in her locker. She'd had her father drop her off in the exact spot as the day before, then slowly followed the same path to school from the SUV, past the giant solar tracking panels that helped power the school, up the front steps, and to her locker. She'd found a ruler, a hair clip, and a tofu-and-banana sandwich—*interesting*—but no diary.

Zee pulled out the textbooks she'd placed on the top shelf, and flipped through the pages for the hundredth time. Discouraged, she shut her locker with a soft *thud*. Like the other lockers at Brookdale, it was made out of boards from recycled wheat straw. She stared at the golden-colored door, trying to figure out what to do next.

"Lose something?" a voice behind Zee asked.

"Iyeee!" Zee screamed as she spun around, her heart pounding from the surprise. Chloe stared back at Zee, a bright pink cello case strapped to her like a backpack. "Sorry, I didn't mean to scare you."

Zee put her hand on her racing heart. "I didn't know anyone else was here."

"My parents made me come early because I missed music yesterday," Chloe explained. "They wanted my nanny to walk me to class today—until she convinced them I was too old for it. That would have been embarrassing."

"Definitely not cool." Zee giggled. "I'll go with you." She picked up her guitar case, which she had stenciled to look like a flag, from the floor beside her. The girls headed to their first-period class.

"What's *your* excuse for getting here so early?" Chloe asked.

"Actually you were right. I did lose something," Zee explained. She told Chloe all about the missing diary and how she was clueless about where it could be. "I'm scared that someone found it and read it."

"Well, you shouldn't freak about it until you know," Chloe told her. "Maybe someone already found it and will give it back today. You're probably worried about nothing."

Everything Chloe said was pretty obvious—and pretty positive! Chloe's attitude was contagious, and Zee decided not to worry as they entered the classroom. Instead, when Chloe started pulling her bow across the cello strings, Zee tuned her guitar and then began practicing her *Teen Sing* song.

Zee strummed the song she'd worked on at the pool over the summer. *"Jump in the water—it's cooler, baby,"* she sang as Chloe played a classical piece. *"Dive in the water—it's better, baby."*

"That note you're starting on is high." Someone else was in the room. Zee twisted around in her chair to find Mr. P. He looked only slightly less frazzled than he had the day before, and he was clutching his coffee cup like a drowning man holding on to a life preserver.

"I'm sorry," Zee said, bending over to put her guitar in its case.

Mr. P sat down next to her with his own guitar. "You shouldn't stop," he said. "Try this chord." He sang back the song's words in a different key. Somehow Mr. P's gravelly voice made it sound like a totally different song. Zee got a little shiver when he looked at her. "Your turn," he said.

Zee tried the song again—Mr. P's way. She couldn't believe how much better it sounded!

"Cool!" Mr. P said, getting up. "I've got to get ready for class, but you should keep practicing." He turned to Chloe. "You must be my missing mystery student from yesterday. I'd like to hear you play later, too. I bet you have some rock and roll in you. Everyone does."

"Suuure," Chloe said, looking doubtfully at her cello.

"That was unbelievable!" Zee whispered as Mr. P walked to his desk. Chloe nodded but she wasn't smiling. Zee could tell something was wrong. "Don't you like Mr. P?" she asked.

Chloe's expression changed to a forced grin. "I dooo," she said hesitantly. "He's just not what I expected."

Considering Zee expected Mrs. Bradley—a round, serious, fifty-five-year-old woman—to be the teacher, she thought she understood what Chloe meant. As her new friend listened, Zee played and sang.

You know it's too hot to be wearing a frown.
Just get off that towel and start splashing around.
We're already treading water
Just to breathe.
So stop—

Zee adjusted her fingers and tried again.

We're already treading water
Just to breathe.
So come—

"Ugh!" Zee sighed.

"What's wrong?" Mr. P asked, looking up from his work.

"I can't remember the next line."

"Did you write it down?"

"Well . . . yes," Zee said. "But I lost the . . . um . . . notebook—maybe at school."

Mr. P stood up from his desk. "You still have time to check the lost and found before the bell rings. I'll go to the office with you," he said, picking up a sheet of paper. "I have to make some copies there."

"Mackenzie Blue Carmichael!" Mrs. Sayles cheerfully greeted Zee across the long counter in the main office. "What can I do you for?"

"I think I lost something yesterday," Zee explained. "May I look in the lost and found?"

Mrs. Sayles motioned toward a box on the floor near her desk. "Sure. It's right there."

Zee went behind the counter. As she rifled through the container, searching for her diary, Kathi came into the office.

"Good morning, Kathi," Mrs. Sayles said.

"Is Dr. Harrison here?" Kathi asked. Dr. Harrison was the upper school's head of school. Most kids dreaded a trip to the principal's office, but Kathi loved it. She always bragged about how much money her family contributed to Brookdale Academy and how that meant the administration had to pay attention to whatever she said.

"She's expecting you," Mrs. Sayles assured her. "Go right in."

Zee held her breath, hoping Kathi wouldn't notice her as she walked to the private office door. She didn't! Whew! Unfortunately Zee's trip to the lost and found was not so successful. The only items in the box were a couple of iPods, a Nintendo DS, a retainer, and a few phones. She gave up and returned to the music room.

By the time Zee got back to first period, all the students were there. Something was definitely weird. Everyone was staring at the front of the room.

MACKENZIE BLUE WONDERS WHEN
SHE'S GOING TO DEVELOP.
WE DO TOO!

Bold purple letters were printed on the dry erase board.

Mr. P stepped into the room behind her and rushed to erase the note while Zee hurried to her seat. She looked at the ground, but as she passed Landon, she caught his friendly smile out of the corner of her eye. "Develop what?" he said, shrugging.

Jen placed her hand over her mouth to hold back a giggle.

As Zee turned to Chloe, she could see the concerned look on her face. They were both thinking the same thing: Someone had Zee's diary!

Kathi walked into the room and handed Mr. P a late pass. Then she sat in the seat Jen had saved for her.

"What's going on?" Kathi whispered to Jen.

"I'll tell you later."

Zee was sure they were not the only ones who would be talking about it.

7
Rock-and-Roll Teacher

"Okay!" Mr. P got everyone's attention. "Let's warm up." He pointed to Zee, Jasper, and Landon. "You three—stay right there and form a group. I'll get you started."

Next, Mr. P pointed to Kathi, Chloe, Jen, and Marcus. "You four—set up near the piano. You'll work on scales."

All the students took their places, and Mr. P moved between groups. As she played, Zee peeked over at Chloe's group. Jen had set up next to Marcus. Kathi's high violin notes and Chloe's deep cello notes climbed the scales together perfectly. Kathi had been the lower school's star musician. In the talent show, Kathi's amazing solo was always the final performance—the best was saved for last. Now Chloe would definitely be competition. Kathi knew it.

But Zee could see Kathi had a bigger problem. She couldn't decide what to be more upset about—the fact that Chloe was an awesome cello player or the fact that Zee was grouped with Landon. Zee could feel the heat of Kathi's glare across the room.

It was all too much for Kathi. She lost her place and started missing notes. Marcus's piano and Jen's marimba couldn't keep the students together. Before long, no one in their group was playing the same scale.

"All right, everyone," Mr. P said. "Nice job."

O-kay, Zee thought. *I'd hate to hear what a terrible job sounds like.* She wondered if Mr. P's clone was in the classroom while the actual teacher had taken a coffee break somewhere else.

"Next, we're going to sight-read," he said, passing out sheet music. It was a Coldplay song, and Mr. P had arranged the music for the instruments in the group.

"Cool," Jasper said. He slid his left hand around his bass strings and strummed with his right hand. Zee joined in.

"Oh, great," Kathi groaned, "rock-and-roll oldies." She flicked her hair behind her shoulder and tucked her violin under her chin. "I guess we're lucky it's not Bob Dylan."

Mr. P laughed nervously. "I thought the class would like to play something by someone who isn't dead," he said.

"Then why did you pick Coldplay?" Kathi mumbled too low for Mr. P to hear. "They were dead on arrival."

"Why don't we just get started?" Mr. P said.

Zee suspected the teacher quickly regretted that decision. With such bad timing and so many missed notes, the class sounded horrible. And Zee was a big part of the problem. She felt terrible about what had appeared on the chalkboard and couldn't concentrate. Who had her diary?

The violin typically led the musicians, but hoping to ruin Mr. P's idea, Kathi was suddenly struck with an inability to play well, which made it hard for the others to keep up with their parts.

Luckily Marcus played the melody on the piano, so it wasn't completely a lost cause. Still, Mr. P kept interrupting the group, offering advice, then saying, "Let's try it one more time." Which was actually *fifteen* more times. Finally the teacher stopped conducting. "I think this is a good place to end," he said, practically panting. He looked like he'd run a marathon. Sweaty clumps of hair stuck to his forehead. "We still have some time left before the end of the period, so . . . hang out."

Finally, Zee thought. Now was her chance to do what she'd been dying to do the entire class—plan her strategy.

How to Avoid Becoming the School Joke

1. Put a lock on your diary.
2. Don't bring your diary to school.
3. Never write down your secrets.

Zee stopped writing. It was no use. Someone already had her diary, so the list couldn't help her now. She sighed and looked up from her paper. Kathi was rushing to the front of the room.

"I have a few suggestions for making the group sound better," she told Mr. P.

"You do?" Mr. P asked, but he didn't sound surprised at all.

Kathi launched into her recommendations. As Zee focused on solving her diary problem, she overheard only bits of what Kathi said. "Students' choice." "Better music." "Mrs. Bradley's way." "All percussion warm up with the strings."

And Zee's personal favorite—"No guitars." It was enough to distract Zee from her troubles and listen.

"Kathi, it's only the second day," Mr. P said. "You can't expect the group to sound like the New York Philharmonic."

Way to go, Mr. P! Zee thought.

"We never will sound like them if we keep playing bad rock music," Kathi told him.

Mr. P sighed and leaned against his desk. His hand landed on top of a folder that slipped out from under him and slid to the floor. Lots of postcards spilled out.

Kathi huffed, then bent down to help clean up the scattered cards. But instead of just handing over the stack she collected, she stuck one inside her music folder.

Mr. P stood up with his own pile of cards. "Sorry, Kathi," he apologized, scratching his head. "What were you saying?"

The bell rang over their heads. "Never mind," Kathi said, turning to leave.

Zee and Chloe huddled near their gym lockers. "I don't understand why gym hasn't been banned as cruel and unusual punishment," Zee said, holding up her school-issued gym uniform—a light blue T-shirt and dark blue shorts. "I mean, who looks good in *this*?" She shuddered.

Chloe laughed. "Yeah, I guess whoever designed it was more concerned about fitness than fashion."

"Why?" Zee asked, baffled.

"Do you really hate gym that much?" Chloe bent over to tie her black running shoe.

"In a word? Yes." Zee eyed the tall locker in front of her. "I wonder if getting stuck in a locker would be an excused absence. Maybe I could pay an eighth grader to shove me in."

"You would rather spend the entire class in a dark locker than take gym?"

"Wouldn't everyone?"

"Not hardly. It's my favorite period," Chloe said.

Zee patted her friend on the shoulder. "Good. You can catch all the balls that come at me. I just wish you could do my push-ups, too."

"At least you still have your sense of humor. I thought you might be more upset about your diary," Chloe said sympathetically.

"I am—a little—but I'm trying to think about my *Teen Sing* audition instead," Zee said. "Mr. P is so awesome. He really helped me a lot this morning."

"Yeah, he knows a lot about rock music," Chloe said halfheartedly.

Zee was surprised when Kathi, already dressed for gym, slid on to the bench right next to her. Jen took the seat beside Chloe. *Ohmylanta!* Zee thought. How could Kathi make those horrible shorts and T-shirt look so good? It just wasn't fair.

"Are you guys talking about the message on Mr. P's board?" Kathi asked.

Oh, *that's why she's here*, Zee thought. *To humiliate me more*.

"Jen told me what it said. You must be so upset. I mean, you don't have boobs, but who cares?"

Zee could feel the heat rise to her cheeks.

"Whatcha got there?" Chloe asked and pointed to the card between Kathi's perfectly manicured fingers. Zee was grateful to her friend for the distraction.

"Oh, just something *very interesting* I found out today in Mr. P's class." Kathi slapped the card down on the bench next to Zee.

"'The Crew,'" Chloe read out loud. "'Live at the Brookdale Amphitheater.'"

Kathi pointed to a photo underneath—five men wearing T-shirts and blue jeans. "Recognize the guy in the middle?" Kathi asked.

Chloe half stood and bent over to get a closer look, but

Zee didn't need to. She recognized Mr. P from her seat. "Mr. P's in a band?" she said, looking from one girl to the next. "Why didn't he tell us?"

"He's probably afraid he's not cool enough," Kathi said. "They're playing the first night of the Brookdale Fall Music Festival in three weeks. I think we should go."

"Me, too," Jen added. "I've never known a real rock musician."

"I have," Kathi said. "But I still think it would be cool to see him. Are you in?"

Zee was confused. She was sure Kathi would rather wear clothes from last season than go to a concert with her. But before Zee could figure out what Kathi was up to, Chloe said, "That could be really awesome. I'll go."

"Great!" Kathi said. "What about you, Zee? I'm sure Mr. P would want his *favorite student* there."

As Zee pulled on her retro gym socks—white knee-highs with two blue stripes at the top—something just didn't feel right. For the past two days, Kathi had

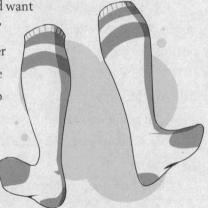

shown absolutely no interest in supporting their teacher. Why now?

"Do you even like Mr. P?" Zee asked.

Kathi's mouth dropped open. She looked shocked and wounded. "I never said I didn't like him," she defended herself. "Maybe I'll understand his style better if I hear him play. My dad is a business manager for *a lot* of celebrities." Chloe looked impressed, but Zee had heard Kathi brag about how important her father was a million times—now a million and one. "He always says you have to separate the music from the rest of the person's life."

"That makes sense to me!" Chloe said.

Kathi ignored her and looked at Zee. "Will you come?"

Zee wasn't sure. Something seemed fishy, but she didn't want to abandon Chloe since she knew how nasty Kathi could be. Plus, it had been so cool to hear Mr. P sing her song. She'd love to watch him perform his own music.

"Okay," Zee said. "I'll go."

Kathi, Jen, and Chloe cheered. "Mr. P might get nervous if he knew we were coming," Kathi said. "Let's keep it a secret and make it a big surprise."

"Great idea!" Jen said.

"I can keep a secret," Chloe agreed.

As a whistle screeched in the gymnasium, Zee felt uncomfortable. She wasn't sure if it was because her least favorite class was about to begin—or because Kathi was suddenly being so nice to her.

8

Party Time

Hi, New Diary,

I know what you're thinking—that I've given up on finding Old Diary. I haven't. Until I find Old Diary, I need a place to keep everything I write. You're it. So I decorated a binder with lots of numbers and squiggly symbols and equations. Then I wrote "Math" on it—just in case. (Who would want to snoop in my math binder?)

It's been ten days since someone wrote that embarrassing message on Mr. P's board. (But who's counting?) No one has brought it up since then, but I can't help but wonder why. Here's what I've come up with:

1. Whoever did it didn't get the reaction they wanted. (That's what my mom thinks.)
2. No one took my diary and the note was just a coincidence. (Too much to hope for?)
3. I have a fairy godmother who cast a spell over Brookdale Academy and made everyone forget everything. (Waaaayyyy too much to hope for.)

Actually I've got more important things to worry about. Like Teen Sing. Mr. P has been helping me with my audition. My song sounds AMAZING! At first, I was playing like I was making a CD—kind of boring. He gave me tips on singing for an audience, which he knows all about since he's in a band. (Which he still doesn't know I know.)

Tonight is Marcus's party. I know it's going to be awesome. Because Landon will be there! Do you think he'll ask me to dance? I know . . . dream on. Maybe I'll ask him to dance. Uhhhhh . . . never mind. (I'm too chicken.)

Cluck cluck,
Zee

* * *

Ding-dong.

"I've got it!" Zee yelled, bounding down the stairs to answer her front door. Chloe stood on the other side, wearing a cool red hoodie over a white T-shirt with a pair of gray capri pants. She had a red bandana tied on top of her head. It was the first time that Zee had seen her friend in something besides her school uniform. Chloe's clothes were plainer than what Zee liked to wear, but Chloe's sporty style looked great on her. Zee still hadn't decided what she was going to wear to Marcus's.

"Crisis!" Zee said, grabbing Chloe's arm. She dragged her friend upstairs to her bedroom, where it looked like a dresser had exploded. About ten different outfits lay across the bed, chair, and desk. Zee picked one up. "What do you think?"

Chloe looked around at the room. Posters of Zee's favorite band—The Jonas Brothers—covered the peach walls. One of them was actually signed in bold black marker,

Zee, keep on rockin'!

Nick.

Chloe's jaw dropped. Before she could say anything, Zee said, "You're right—this outfit is all wrong." Zee scooped shirts, skirts, pants, leggings, and dresses in her arms and tossed them in a heap on the chair in the corner.

"The Jonas Brothers is my favorite band, too! I can't be-lieve—" Chloe started to say, but Zee had already stepped into her closet and started all over again. She *had* to choose the perfect party outfit. Landon would be there.

Zee slid hangers across the closet rod, rejecting some clothes—too frilly, too plain, too *much*—and tossing others into the maybe pile on her bed. "Have you been to the mall yet?" she asked Chloe as she searched.

"No," Chloe said. "My mom's crazy with a big case. As soon as she wins it—which she will since she always does—she's gonna take me."

"You can go with my mom and me if you want. There is *the most* amazing store there. I practically live in it. I mean . . . not when it's closed . . . and actually I'm here now, so I'm not there all the time, but I really like it." Zee exited the closet to dig through the top drawer of the dresser and look for her peach tank top. She knew she'd put it in there the day before. "My mom and I always get a Frappuccino before we come home."

Chloe licked her lips. "Yum," she said as Zee triumphantly pulled the shirt out of the drawer.

"You're going to love Brookdale," Zee told her. "I do." Zee zipped past the stack of clothes on her bed and over to her closet. "Where did I put that dress?" she mumbled, then got down on her hands and knees to search the closet floor. "Am I talking a lot again?"

"Uh-huh," Chloe said. "But I don't have any brothers or sisters, so I don't mind a *teeny* bit."

Zee slowly got up with the dress she was looking for clutched in her hand. The ball of blue-green-and-purple-striped fabric slowly unrolled. "Awesome!" Chloe's face lit up as the dress fell to knee length, revealing thin blue straps at the top.

Zee quickly pulled on the tank top and dived into the dress. Her arms grabbed and flailed as the loose material wrapped around her and she searched for the hole to stick her head through.

"Is that a tattoo?" Chloe asked.

"What?" Zee asked.

"By your elbow. It looks like a heart."

Zee's head popped out of the top of the dress. "It's my birthmark."

"You were born with a heart-shaped birthmark? That is *so* awesome."

"Yeah, I'm lucky it looks like a heart instead of a skull and crossbones."

Chloe laughed. "Speaking of hearts," she began slowly, "I think Jasper likes you."

Zee tripped on a pair of pants that was lying on the floor, and she nearly fell on her face. "No way," she protested. "We're just friends."

"Okay. Whatever you say," Chloe said skeptically and rushed to the sink in the bathroom connected to Zee's bedroom. Her eyes widened as she looked at the plastic bins lined up on the counter. "Wow! Do your parents buy you all this makeup?" she asked.

"No, that's stuff my dad gets for free at his office. He works at *Gala*."

"The magazine?" Chloe asked. Zee nodded. "Do you get to meet lots of celebrities?"

"Sometimes—like at a movie premiere or something. Mostly I just get free stuff nobody else wants. The makeup's just for fun anyway. I'm not even allowed to wear it to school."

Chloe picked up a tube of lipstick. "Can you wear it tonight?"

"According to my father, I can as long as I don't look like a clown," Zee said.

"But that's such an awesome look," Chloe joked. She popped the lid off the lipstick and twisted it so that the rose sunset tip peeked out. "Pucker up. I promise you won't look like a clown."

Zee stuck out her lips so Chloe could apply the color. Then she studied herself in the mirror. "My mom said she'd do my makeup for the *Teen Sing* audition."

"Your mom must be amazing. I don't think mine will *ever* let me wear makeup—except maybe on my wedding day." Chloe snapped the cap back on the tube. "I'm not sure I really want to wear it anyway. Some companies use animals to test makeup."

"But animals don't wear makeup!" Zee exclaimed. "Except maybe the ones on TV and in movies."

Chloe laughed. "You're so funny, Zee."

Zee giggled—even though she hadn't meant to make a joke. "Why do they test on animals anyway?" she asked.

"Some companies use animals to make sure their products won't hurt humans," Chloe explained. "But other companies get the same information without using animals."

"So why would you hurt animals if you don't have to?" asked Zee.

"That's exactly my point!" Chloe said, nodding enthusiastically. "Companies also put animal ingredients in makeup sometimes. Like, I bet this lipstick has cow parts in it."

"Yuck!" Zee squealed, wiping her lips with the back of her hand and making a *pppppft pppppft* sound as she tried to get the lipstick off her lips.

"I know," Chloe drawled, then quickly added, "Not all of them do it though."

"Next time I go to my dad's office, I'll definitely bring you, too, so you can help me pick out the makeup that doesn't have weird stuff in it."

"Wouldn't it be so cool if we made our own line of animal-friendly cosmetics?" Chloe said, searching through Zee's basket of eye shadow.

"Chlo-Zee's!" Zee suggested.

"Oh *my* gosh! That's so awesome," Chloe agreed.

The doorbell rang. "Jasper!" the girls exclaimed and headed toward Zee's bedroom door. Mr. Carmichael was going to take the three of them over to Marcus's house.

"I'll get it!" Zee shouted down to the first floor.

"Incoming!" Zee's father yelled as she practically flew downstairs, with Chloe close behind.

"Hi, Dad!" Zee said, shooting past her father. "This is Chloe."

"Hello, Mr. Carmichael," Chloe said, stopping in front of him.

"It's nice to—" Zee grabbed her friend by the arm and pulled her toward the door. "—errr . . . *was* nice to meet you," Mr. Carmichael said.

Zee opened the door. Jasper stood there with an eager smile on his face. "I'm ready for my first American party."

"Come on in," Zee told Jasper. As usual, he was wearing a collared short-sleeve button-down shirt neatly tucked into his belted tan chino pants. "I'll give you ten dollars if you pull out the tail of your shirt."

"No, thank you," Jasper replied casually. "I like it this way. It's how I always dress for parties."

"Yes, but when in Rome . . . ," Zee said.

"We're not in Rome," Jasper pointed out. "We're in Brookdale."

"Are you guys ready to go?" Mr. Carmichael asked.

Zee looked at him as though he had just grown a horn right in the middle of his forehead. "It's way too early."

"But it's five o'clock. The party's starting now."

"Right. We don't want to be the first ones. We can go in thirty minutes," Zee told him.

"Okay, but I need to take you then. Believe it or not, I have my own life to live and I'd like to get on with it sometime tonight."

Chloe giggled as Mr. Carmichael left the room. "Your dad is funny."

Zee gave Chloe a sideways look. "Please don't ever tell him that. It'll only make him harder to live with."

"I heard that!" Zee's dad called from the other room. "And thanks, Chloe."

"My pleasure, Mr. Carmichael."

"Let's go to the TV room," Zee said, "before Chloe gets dragged farther over to the dark side."

Chloe followed, walking stiffly with her arms out straight. "Errrrg. Arrrr." She sounded like a zombie with a Southern accent.

"So have you guys decided what you're going to do for your science project?" Zee asked.

Chloe looked at Jasper. Jasper looked at Chloe. Neither one looked at Zee. Finally Chloe said, "We've decided not to tell anyone."

"Oh," Zee said, completely surprised. Her new friends had a secret—and they didn't want to tell her.

"It's just that we're still working on it and might change our minds," Jasper explained. He nervously picked up the

remote control and pointed it at the television. "I need to check the football—uh . . . soccer—score," he said, pushing buttons.

"Do you play?" Chloe asked.

"No, but I'm a huge fan of Manchester United."

"Did you ever see David Beckham when he played for them?" Zee asked Jasper. The only thing she knew about soccer was that David Beckham was the cutest player. Ever. In the history of the sport. But Zee was feeling left out. So maybe talking about sports would help her fit in.

"No, but I can't wait to go to a Galaxy game and watch him," Jasper said.

"Me, too!" Chloe jumped in. "That's the most awesome part of living near Los Angeles."

Zee could think of ten (maybe one hundred) other things that were more awesome about living near LA—like Beverly Hills boutiques, the downtown shopping district's sample sales, celebrity sightings, the rides on Santa Monica Pier, the beach, and constant sunshine. But she didn't want to highlight the fact that she had no interest in Chloe's and Jasper's favorite sport.

Mrs. Carmichael entered the room with a big tray of snacks. "Don't mind me," she told them. "I just didn't want you to get hungry before the party."

"Thank you, Mrs. Carmichael!" Jasper said.

"Oh, you're welcome, Jasper," Zee's mom gushed, setting the tray on the table before she left the room.

"So spill. What's the scoop on the seventh-grade boys?" Chloe asked, plopping herself down on the couch so hard she bounced up and down. "Who's hot and who's not?"

"*Definitely* time for me to watch the telly," Jasper said.

"Yeah, we've already got you figured out," Chloe told him.

"Undoubtedly," Jasper said, turning to face the TV.

"Is that how everyone talks in England?" Chloe asked. Zee sometimes wondered about that, too. With his books and clothes, Jasper wasn't like the other seventh-grade boys. And she had never had a friend who was so different from her. He was quiet, and she was talkative. He spoke like a professor, and she sounded like a student. He dressed to hide in a crowd. She stood out. But they were great friends.

"So how about the guys?" Chloe coaxed.

"They're okay," Zee said, trying to sound casual. "Marcus is really cool."

"What about his best friend, Landon?" Chloe asked. "He's cute."

Zee's water shot out of her mouth like a Super Soaker.

"Nice!" Jasper said sarcastically, sounding *just like* a seventh grader.

"What was *that* about?" Chloe asked.

"Nothing," Zee said quickly. "It just went down the wrong way."

"Looks like it didn't go down at all," Jasper said. "I'm glad I got out of the line of fire—mostly." He wiped water droplets off his clothes.

"Landon's nice." Zee tried to sound cool. Chloe was getting to be a good friend, but Zee wasn't ready to tell her about her crush on Landon. She hadn't even told Jasper yet.

Zee's brother looked in the room. "Adam!" she shouted enthusiastically, hoping to change the subject. She waved her hand in the air. "Come on in!"

With a suspicious look on his face, Adam took a step forward. "Looks like you've survived the first couple of weeks of seventh grade," he said to the threesome. "I guess the eighth graders decided to go easy on you."

"Ohmylanta!" Zee groaned. "Yes, your predictions that we'd get flushed down a toilet haven't come true."

"Give it time," he warned them. "The worst is probably still coming."

"What do you mean?" Chloe asked.

"When I was an eighth grader, we took the seventh graders' clothes out of their gym lockers and put them in the courtyard."

"Do Mom and Dad know?" Zee asked.

"No—just like they don't know you're the one who tried to play a piece of cheese in the DVD player."

"Good point," Zee said. "But I think that if the eighth graders had something planned, they would have done it by now."

Adam pulled his car keys out of his pocket and headed out of the room. "Fine—don't believe me," he called behind him. "But don't come crying to me when you need help. I'm outta here." His voice trailed off as he disappeared from sight.

Chloe turned to Zee with wide eyes. "That's it!"

"*What's* it?" Zee asked.

"You kinda *were* tortured—by the note on the music room board," Chloe pointed out. "Maybe an eighth grader did it."

"Maybe an eighth grader took your diary," Jasper added.

Were Adam's stories about eighth-grade torture real? Zee had figured her brother was just messing with her. But Chloe and Jasper made a lot of sense.

Chloe sprang out of her seat. "I have to go to the bathroom," she explained as she headed toward the stairs.

"You can use the one down here," Zee told her.

Chloe kept moving in the same direction. "I already know where yours is," she said. "I'll be right back."

While Chloe was gone, Mr. Carmichael came into the room and announced that it was time to go. "Anyone who's not ready will have to stay here and cook me dinner."

"I'll let Chloe know!" Zee volunteered. As she climbed the steps to the second floor hallway, she heard a door shut. She figured Chloe was on her way downstairs. But when Zee turned the corner into her room, Chloe was standing in the middle of it, looking confused and flustered, and the bathroom door wasn't shut. *That's weird*, Zee thought. "What are you doing?" she asked.

"Oh . . . just getting my stuff. Woo-hoo! Let's party!" Chloe said. The girls grabbed their swim bags—complete with suits and towels—ready to have fun.

9

Text Trouble

"*C*annonball!" A blur raced down the diving board and bounced off the end. *Boing! Splash!* Zee was standing too close to the pool and now her bathing suit, a periwinkle-colored bikini with white embroidered flowers, was wet.

Jasper popped out from behind Zee, where he had ducked for cover. "My hero," Zee said sarcastically.

"I'm not wearing a swimming costume," Jasper said defensively.

"What's a swimming costume?" Chloe asked. She was wearing shorts over a one-piece with a bold red-and-blue tie-dye sunburst.

"It's a bathing suit," Zee said.

Jasper smiled sheepishly. "I didn't expect to have to learn a new language when I moved here."

The party was even better than Zee had imagined. Kids were swarming everywhere, eating burgers, playing video games on the biggest TV Zee had ever seen, and even shooting hoops on the Montgomerys' indoor basketball court.

Chloe grabbed Jasper's arm and pulled him away from the side of the pool. "Come on!" she said, wiggling her hips. "Loosen up."

Zee, Chloe, and Jasper had been hanging out on the patio, listening to the band. Chloe hadn't stopped dancing since they'd gotten there.

Jasper moved his head up and down like a bobblehead doll. "I am *quite* loose."

Zee tilted her head sideways to study him. "This *is* pretty loose for him," she told Chloe.

Marcus came over to the three friends. "Are you having fun?" he asked, putting an arm around Zee and Chloe.

"Yes! This band is incredible!" Chloe told him.

"Where did you find them?" Zee asked.

"At UCLA," Marcus shouted over the noise. "My mother teaches one of them." He grabbed the girls' hands and pulled them to the center of the dance floor. As they danced, Zee looked around at all of the people she didn't know. Marcus

had four brothers and sisters, and they had invited their own friends. A few bodies collided into Zee, but she was having so much fun, she didn't care.

There was just one problem keeping the party from being perfect. Kathi. She had managed to hog Landon all to herself. She even got him to dance the slow dances with her. Jen hovered nearby, looking like an awkward dancing shadow. When the band finally took a break, Zee wondered how she was going to get Landon away from Kathi.

Marcus solved her problem. "I have an idea," he announced.

"Everyone who is competing in *Teen Sing* should perform here."

"Tonight?" Zee asked, a rush of terror zipping from her toes to her forehead. "My song isn't ready yet."

"That's okay," Marcus assured her. "You can sing whatever you want. It's just for fun."

"I guess I could sing 'Umbrella,'" Zee mumbled to herself.

"Rihanna?" Marcus said. "Cool. You can go first."

First? Yikes! "Maybe you should let someone else go," Zee blurted.

"But you said you'd sing it," Jasper pointed out. True. But she had never performed it without shampoo in her hair and a showerhead in her hand.

Chloe gave Zee an encouraging tug on her arm. "Oh, I'm just dying to hear you. Please. For your friends?"

By now, Landon, Kathi, and Jen had joined the others. "Yeah," Landon said with a friendly smile. "We're here for you."

That was all the encouragement Zee needed. "Okay," she said as she stepped up to the microphone. There was no band, no chorus, no one to back her up. Her legs trembled a little as she opened her mouth to sing.

At first, Zee sang a little quietly, then as she repeated

the words, a few kids joined in. She watched more and more kids sing along, and she smiled as she noticed Jasper actually begin stepping to the beat. Once nearly everyone had joined in, she moved on. And let loose.

Zee hit every note. The words flowed out. All eyes focused on her as she built up to her favorite part, her voice getting stronger and climbing louder. "'*So go on and let the rain pour, I'll be all you need and more.*'" It was so much easier than she'd imagined.

When Zee finished, the crowd clapped and cheered. Shrill whistles pierced the other noise. She looked over the rest of the audience to Chloe and Jasper. Chloe was jumping up and down excitedly, and Jasper was nodding his head and smiling.

Zee left the stage. "Way to go!" one of Marcus's brothers said.

"That was great!" a Brookdale sophomore told her.

The compliments continued as she passed through the party. Finally Zee reached her friends, who were standing near the pool. Chloe threw her arms around her. "You are *so* going to win *Teen Sing*."

Landon moved closer to Zee. "I knew you were good, but I didn't know how good," he told her. "Maybe you can help me with *my* singing sometime." *Whoosh!* A rush of heat filled Zee, and she wondered if it were possible for a person to spontaneously combust.

"Sure," Zee agreed, afraid if she said any more she'd embarrass herself.

"My turn," Kathi said, pushing past. Before Zee knew it, she had lost her balance. *Ker-splash!* She landed backward in the pool.

Kathi bent over. "Oh, I'm such a klutz," she told Zee, without bothering to offer a hand.

Jasper stepped in front of Kathi and reached toward Zee, soaked from her big splash. "I had no idea this would be such a dangerous party," he said. Zee couldn't help laughing as water rolled down his face. Luckily neither could Jasper.

As Zee climbed out of the pool, Kathi took the stage. She sang like she was born to be there. Every note was perfect, and Kathi looked totally natural. Zee had competition!

After a few other kids took turns, Marcus turned to Chloe and Zee. "Hey, Chloe! You should go next," he said. "Brookdale's never heard you sing before."

"That's an awesome idea!" Zee exclaimed. "Go for it!"

"Really?" Chloe gulped and looked at her group of friends, who stared back expectantly. She looked sick.

As Chloe's face got paler, Zee regretted mentioning anything.

Then Kathi turned to Jen and fake-whispered, "She's probably scared."

"I think she's going to spew," Jen said.

Chloe's expression went from terrified to determined. "I'll do it!" she said boldly. But as Chloe stepped up to the microphone, her legs looked like noodles. Zee braced for disaster and closed her eyes.

"'*Ooh-ooh*.'" Chloe began singing so quietly her friends could barely tell which song she had chosen. But then all of a sudden—*poof!*—Chloe's nerves seemed to evaporate. She started clapping her hands together, then motioned for the rest of the party to join in. "'*When you left, I lost a part of me,*'" Chloe dived into the chorus of the Mariah Carey classic "We Belong Together" as her friends kept the beat. And best of all, she looked like she was having an amazing time. She couldn't stand still. And neither could anyone else.

When Chloe finished singing the last note, Zee couldn't wait. She rushed up onto the stage. "You were so great! You should audition for *Teen Sing*," she suggested—even though Zee knew that Chloe would be even more competition.

Chloe bit her lip. "Maybe," she said weakly.

"Are you okay?" Zee asked. Had she said something wrong?

"I think I just need some water," Chloe said, rushing away.

The band returned to the stage. "Awesome singing!" the lead singer told Zee.

"Thanks," Zee said absentmindedly, her eyes on Chloe.

Zee moved through the maze of people, looking for Jasper. She stopped when her Sidekick beeped with a text message.

>Have u found ur diary?

She didn't recognize the phone number. That was strange—the only people who knew about the missing diary were Ally, Jasper, Chloe, and her family.

"What's wrong?" Chloe asked, coming to Zee's side. She took a sip from the big red cup in her hand.

Zee showed Chloe the text message. "I don't know who it's from," she said.

"Do you think it's a threat?" Chloe asked.

"What else could it be?" Zee wondered.

"It might just be a friendly question," Chloe said sweetly, "from someone who's concerned."

Zee had to admit, she hadn't thought of that. Still, the mysterious number just didn't make sense. "Maybe," Zee said doubtfully.

✳ ✳ ✳

10 Ways to Know Who Your Enemies Are

Zee held the pen over the blank page, then finally gave up and shut her diary. Who had sent her the mysterious text the night before? She had no suspects. No clue who could be torturing her. Maybe Chloe was right and it was an eighth grader. Or maybe Chloe was right and it was nobody.

 E-ZEE: Bonjour! Ça va?

 SPARKLEGRRL: LOL. Ur learning French fast.

 E-ZEE: I can't w8 2 visit and do all the cool stuff ur doing.

SPARKLEGRRL: 2day M, D, & I r going to Ladurée.

 E-ZEE: ?

 SPARKLEGRRL: It's a tea shop—even tho I'd rather have a Frap. They make delish macaroons tho. Raspberry is my fave.

 E-ZEE: Mmmmm.

 SPARKLEGRRL: It's not all mmmmm. 2day I 8 escargot, which is a fancy way 2 say snails. DISGUSTING!!!!!

 E-ZEE: Yuck!

 SPARKLEGRRL: I had 2 pretend 2 like it so the French kids would like me. Then I made my parents take me 2 McDonald's. LOL!

E-ZEE: There must b lots of other stuff to eat.

 SPARKLEGRRL: I wouldn't know. I'm afraid 2 order anything because I don't know what it is. I feel like a freak here.

 E-ZEE: I know what u mean.

 SPARKLEGRRL: Y?

 E-ZEE: I had a great time at Marcus's party, but I got a weird text.

Zee told her about the message.

 SPARKLEGRRL: Who sent it?

 E-ZEE: That's the problem. idk. <Sigh>

Zee typed, *Mayb u can help me come up with a list of*

suspects, but before she could send it, Ally wrote,

 SPARKLEGRRL: Mom is calling me. We're going to Le Bon Marché.

 E-ZEE: Translate pls.

 SPARKLEGRRL: Shopping. It's a huge old store. I hope she lets me get those high heels I've been begging 4. It's the only way I'll ever fit in. ARFN.

 E-ZEE: K. ARFN.

How could Ally think about shoes at a time like this?

Teacher Feature

Hi, Diary,

It's hard having my BFF so far away. When we were both in Brookdale, we could talk about our problems and go shopping together. Now we can only talk when we're on the computer at the same time—and Ally's not too busy. It's not her fault, but it still stinks.

I may not have my best friend, but I definitely have my friends. Tonight is the Crew concert. Kathi, Jen, Chloe, and I have been planning it all week. Kathi keeps calling it our "girls' night out." She calls us "the gang." I know Kathi gave Mr. P a hard time and thinks she's God's gift to Brookdale Academy. But it's more fun being a part of a group. And being with them distracts me from my diary—the other diary—problems.

Zee

* * *

Adam stuck his head into Zee's bedroom as she was snipping the last uneven hairs from her bangs.

"Please, please don't embarrass me," Zee said to her brother's reflection in her mirror.

"Don't you think *I* should be telling *you* that?" Adam asked.

"No," Zee answered, putting down the scissors on her cream-colored vanity.

The night of the Brookdale Fall Music Festival had finally arrived. Zee, Chloe, Kathi, and Jen had planned where they'd meet up, what they'd wear, and where they'd sit—right near the stage, thanks to the people Kathi's dad knew.

"Remember our deal," Zee told her brother as she slipped on a pair of hoop earrings. "You sit on the lawn for the concert. At all other times, keep at least ten feet back."

Adam leaned against the door frame. "No problem. As cool as it would be to hang out with a bunch of seventh graders," he said sarcastically, "I know when I'm not wanted."

Zee turned around in her chair. "It's not that you're not wanted," she said. "Tonight's just a big deal for me. I want to hang out with my friends and not feel like I have a chaperone."

"C'mon. You're lucky Mom and Dad let me take you

instead of them. I promise not to act like a parent," Adam said.

"Or . . . ?" Zee coaxed.

"Or a big brother."

"Thanks."

Outside, Zee opened the door to Adam's car. She carefully picked up an old cheese-globbed burger wrapper and added it to the collection in the backseat. There was no way she was going to mess up her brand-new denim miniskirt— Dad said it was okay to wear since she had on a pair of leggings underneath—because of her brother's revolting habits. "You know, they actually make trash cans now," Zee said.

"If you'd rather not get a ride, that's okay with me," Adam said.

"No, it's fine," she told him. "I'll just avoid making contact with any surfaces."

As Zee buckled her seat belt, she got a text message. "It's Chloe," she told her brother.

"We're not late, are we?"

Zee read the message. "We don't need to pick her up for the concert."

"Why not?"

Zee stared at the words—

>I can't go 2nite. Sorry.

"She didn't say." Frustrated, Zee dropped her Sidekick into her purse and stared at the car window. Why couldn't Chloe go? she wondered. Half the time, Zee could almost read Ally's mind—and the other half of the time, Ally told her *everything*. It was different with Chloe. Was she hiding something from Zee?

Just as the girls had discussed, Kathi and Jen were waiting by the main gate. Even from a distance, Zee could see the passes, spread out like a fan, in Kathi's hands.

"I loooooove your hair!" Kathi said as Zee got close. Zee turned around to look behind her, but besides Adam, no one else was there.

"Me?" Zee asked, pointing to herself.

"Of course, you," Kathi said. "Who else would I mean?"

Everybody, Zee thought. Although Kathi had been way nicer to her over the past week, she had never complimented Zee's style before.

"I've always admired the color," Kathi said. "It's . . . " She turned to Jen.

"Vivid," Jen said. "Like a penny!"

"Exactly." Kathi nodded and smiled. Then she looked around. "Where's Chloe?"

"She couldn't come," Zee explained.

"Why not?" Kathi asked.

"I don't know," Zee said.

"Didn't she tell you?" Kathi pressed.

"No."

"You're like her best friend." Kathi made a face like she'd just bitten into a lemon. "Don't you think that's weird?"

Zee did, but how could she say that? Chloe was her friend—at least she thought so. "I . . . uh . . . don't think she had time."

Kathi handed Jen and Zee their tickets, then walked over toward where Adam was standing—ten feet away. "Oh no!" Zee shouted, chasing after her. "He has his own ticket for the lawn."

"He might as well use Chloe's ticket since she's not here," Kathi said, flashing him a princess-perfect smile. "Besides,

seniors shouldn't have to sit on the lawn."

From behind Kathi's and Jen's backs, Zee looked at her brother and stiffly shook her head in an urgent no. Adam plucked the ticket from Kathi's hand. "Thank you, Kathi." Then he whispered to Zee, "You don't expect me to pass up a front row seat, do you?"

"Yes!" Zee hissed back, her eyes growing wide with panic.

"I'll make it up to you. I promise."

"Let's go get some food before we sit down," Kathi suggested.

"Great idea!" Adam said.

As they walked toward the concession stand, Zee nudged Adam in the ribs.

Adam got the hint. "Get me some buffalo wings!" he called out, dropping behind. "With extra sauce." Zee gave him a thumbs-up.

When the girls got to the food line, Kathi turned to Zee and said, "You must have been soooo embarrassed by that note on the music room board." Zee felt herself turn bright red. After all this time, she had thought everyone had forgotten about the note. It figured that Kathi would bring it up. "Why would someone write that?" Kathi asked. "It was really mean."

"Well . . . uh . . . ummm," Zee stammered, trying to find

a way to avoid telling Kathi it was a quote from her diary. "I don't know." *Duh*.

"I'm just glad nobody's done anything else to you."

"Actually . . . ," Zee began, "I think someone took my diary the first day of school."

Jen gasped.

"No way," Kathi said. "That's awful."

Zee told Kathi and Jen about the text she had gotten at Marcus's party.

"That must have ruined your *whole* evening," Kathi said. "Who do you think it was?"

Zee shook her head. "I don't know, but—"

Kathi cut Zee off. "*I* think it was Chloe."

"Yeah," Jen said. "She's new *and* she carries a homemade bag."

Huh? It was the weirdest reason Zee had ever heard for accusing someone of theft. Owning a glue gun didn't make Chloe a criminal! "Well . . . I think Chloe's bag is really cool. I decorated mine, too," Zee said.

Kathi gave Jen a disgusted look, then stepped in front of her. "Oh, your bag is adorable! But it's just decorated. Chloe's is made from scratch."

Even though Zee didn't get why sewing qualified a person for the FBI's Most Wanted, she didn't feel like arguing. Still, talking about the bags made Zee's mind flash. She had let Chloe hold her bag on the first day of school. Then, the day the note appeared on the whiteboard, Zee and Mr. P had left Chloe all alone in the music room. Did Chloe really have to use Zee's bathroom before Marcus's party, or was she looking for something—to steal?

Zee reached the front of the line and placed her order: "Buffalo wings and french fries, please." Since Mrs. Carmichael almost never let Zee and Adam eat junk food, they looked forward to the chance to eat out and get what they wanted.

Kathi and Jen got their food, too. As they headed back to their seats, Zee recognized a few older students from Brookdale Academy. Of course, Kathi actually *knew* them and talked to them like they were her best friends. The smell from the fries teased Zee's nose, but with her snack in one hand and Adam's in the other, even one bite was impossible. It seemed to take forever to get across the lawn as they creeped from one person to the next. Until finally they were on their way.

"Hey, Kathi!" a voice called out.

Screech! Putting on the brakes, Zee turned to see who Kathi's latest fan was. Marcus! Finally someone *she* knew, too!

"Did Landon come with you?" Kathi wondered. Of course, Zee had the same question, but there was no way she was going to ask.

"No, he heard there were going to be some monster waves tonight, so he's surfing." Zee tried not to let on, but she felt as disappointed as Kathi looked. "I checked out the music blogs," Marcus continued. "Someone said The Crew was amazing, so I got a ticket at the last minute. How'd you find out about the concert?"

Zee looked at the other girls. What would they tell Marcus? They had kept the concert a secret. Zee panicked. "Did you know Mr. P was in the band?" she asked Marcus. Her voice squeaked from the strain of trying to remain calm.

"Mr. P who?" he asked.

"*Our* Mr. P," Zee explained. "Mr. Papademetriou." The panic disappeared a little.

Marcus stepped back. "Are you serious?" he shouted. "That's really cool. Did he tell you about the show?"

Welcome back, Panic. "Well . . . uh . . . umm . . . ," Zee stammered.

"Actually"—Kathi blocked Zee—"*I'm* the one who told her about it. I know the right people."

If Marcus was impressed, he didn't show it. He looked from Kathi to Zee to Jen. "Where's Chloe?" he asked.

"She didn't come," Jen said quickly.

"That's too bad," Marcus said.

Jen pouted and crossed her arms. "Yeah, well, we need to sit down." Which was a relief to Zee since the fries and buffalo wings were getting so heavy they were threatening to abandon ship.

"I'll come with you," Marcus said, looking around the lawn. "Where do you want to sit?"

Kathi waved her ticket in the air. "We're in the front row."

"How'd you get up there?" Marcus asked. "I heard everything except the lawn has been sold out for weeks!"

"It helps if your father is one of LA's top business managers," Kathi reminded him.

"Well, have fun," he said.

Zee said good-bye, then followed Kathi to their seats,

where Adam was waiting and, judging from the way he grabbed for his wings, very hungry.

Before long, the lights went down and the music began.

The Crew was awesome. Zee, Jen, and Kathi were out of their seats dancing almost the entire time. But whenever Adam got up to play air guitar, Zee regretted the great seats. Zee imagined a neon SUPER DORK sign over her brother's head, shining so bright that Ally could see it all the way from Paris. At least it was dark in the amphitheater. Mr. P probably couldn't even see them.

After the concert, the band came to the side of the stage. A crowd quickly swarmed around them.

"Let's go get Mr. P's autograph," Kathi suggested.

"Why don't we just talk to him on Monday?" Zee said. "I don't want to wait behind all these people."

"Who says we're going to wait?" Kathi asked. "Follow me." Zee and Jen did, and Adam stayed close behind. "Excuse me . . . Excuse me," Kathi said as she pushed her way through the fans.

A thrill of excitement rushed through Zee. "Cool beans!" she said.

Jen nodded and leaned toward her. "It's fun to hang out with Kathi," she said. "She knows how to get what she wants."

Of course, getting elbowed and stepped on by the other fans wasn't great, but Zee quickly forgot about her aches and pains when she reached the front.

Zee was right next to Mr. P when a girl Adam's age told him, "You guys were so great. My dream is to be a professional musician—the star of my own band—like you."

Kathi snorted and said, "If you want to be like him, you should consider becoming a music teacher. We're his students." She turned to Zee and Jen. "Right?"

Zee nodded. "Yeah," she said, but it sounded more like a question.

The fan's smile disappeared. "Oh, okay," she said as she took her autograph and walked away.

Zee suddenly felt incredibly uncomfortable. Kathi had ruined Mr. P's moment. Certain she had embarrassed her teacher, too, Zee turned to go. "I'll see you at school on Monday," she told Kathi and Jen. She grabbed Adam's sleeve and pushed back through the fans.

"That was way uncool of Kathi," Adam said as they walked through the parking lot.

"I know," Zee sighed. A sick feeling crawled from her toes to her stomach.

5 Reasons I Should Never
Leave My House

1. I might do the wrong thing.

2. I might say the wrong thing.

3. I might trust the wrong person.

4. I might hurt someone I really like.

5. My brother might play the air guitar and humiliate me in front of some very cool people.

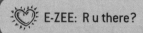 **E-ZEE:** R u there?

 SPARKLEGRRL: What's up?

Zee told her best friend what had happened at the concert—about how the fan practically ran away and the look on Mr. P's face when he saw the three girls. She even told Ally about how Chloe didn't show up for the concert and Kathi's suspicion that Chloe had stolen her diary.

 SPARKLEGRRL: Maybe Chloe was sick.

 E-ZEE: She looked OK @ school.

 SPARKLEGRRL: Just bc she wasn't there doesn't mean she took ur diary. And y would u trust Kathi?

Zee didn't know how to explain. She left Ally's question hanging and changed the subject.

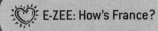 **E-ZEE:** How's France?

 SPARKLEGRRL: I M going 2 my 1st French party 2nite!!!

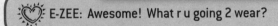 **E-ZEE:** Awesome! What r u going 2 wear?

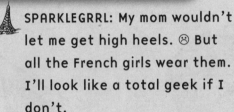 **SPARKLEGRRL:** My mom wouldn't let me get high heels. ☹ But all the French girls wear them. I'll look like a total geek if I don't.

E-ZEE: What r u going 2 do?

SPARKLEGRRL: I borrowed a pair. I'll just change into them after I leave the apartment.

As Zee typed her response, another IM came in. Zee didn't recognize the user name.

 CALIFORNIA12: Where could it b?

E-ZEE: Where could what b?

 CALIFORNIA12: U know. Ur diary.

 E-ZEE: Y r u doing this 2 me?

 CALIFORNIA12: Y not?

 E-ZEE: I never did anything 2 u.

 CALIFORNIA12: Don't be so sure. The big surprise is coming.

 E-ZEE: What surprise?

But the mysterious user logged off before answering Zee's question. As quickly as she could type, Zee told Ally what had happened.

 SPARKLEGRRL: What r u going 2 do?

 E-ZEE: Get my diary back b4 the big surprise.

Yes No

Three Things a Star Needs

1. A great voice.
2. A great song.
3. A great outfit.

Hi, Diary,

I can't wait! Dad's going to take me to his office. They have a bunch of dresses that they use for the magazine's photo shoots, and I get to pick one to wear for the Teen Sing audition. One that a famous movie star—or singer (even better)—wore!

Chloe called to ask about Mr. P's band, which was weird since she didn't ever say why she couldn't go see them. I think she wanted to hang out with me! I told her I didn't have time all weekend because I have to practice and get ready for Teen Sing. Which is totally true. Technically I promised to take Chloe to my dad's offices the next time I went. But that feels too risky now. What if she did take my diary and uses all the personal stuff she's found out to sabotage my audition? What if that's the big surprise?

Zee

"Who wore this one?" Zee asked her father. She modeled a red sequined dress that made swishy sounds when she walked.

"Nicole Richie," Mr. Carmichael said. "That was for a cover."

"I'm the same size as Nicole Richie," Zee said to Jasper.

"Mmm-hmm," Jasper responded.

She'd practically had to *beg* him to come when she'd called him that morning. He'd been working on the Power-Point presentation for his science project and didn't want to stop. But Zee needed backup—someone to take her side when her father said no to a dress she liked. Unfortunately

Zee's plan hadn't worked out very well. Jasper had spent the whole time telling Mr. Carmichael how to make the *Gala* offices more environmentally friendly.

Zee spun around. "So? What do you think?" she asked her father and Jasper.

Mr. Carmichael put his chin in his hand and studied the dress Zee was wearing. Then he matter-of-factly said, "No."

"Dad! This is the tenth dress you've said no to," Zee complained.

"It's the tenth dress that looks much too old for you," he defended himself. "You may be the same size as Nicole Richie, but you're not the same age."

"I'm going to be a teenager in a year."

"Oh, good," Mr. Carmichael said cheerfully. "That gives me twelve whole months while you're still my little girl. Try again."

With pleading eyes that screamed, "Back me up here," Zee turned to Jasper for help. He didn't notice.

"You could put all of the lights on a sensor so they go out if no one is in the room," Jasper was telling Zee's father.

"I wish Mom had come to save me," Zee mumbled as she headed back to the dress racks.

"You could give each employee a reusable coffee mug so they don't have to keep throwing away paper cups," Zee heard Jasper explaining behind her.

"Boy, Jasper, those are great ideas, but I bet Zee could use your help picking out a dress," Mr. Carmichael said. "Why don't you go find something with her?"

"Well . . . okay," Jasper said reluctantly.

Zee giggled. Maybe she should let Jasper torture her father until he agreed to let her wear the dress she wanted.

As Zee searched through the racks of clothes, Jasper began looking around the room. "I wonder if that copier has an energy-saver mode," he said.

"Ummm . . . the dresses are over here," Zee teased.

"Huh?" Jasper turned around. "Oh, I guess I'm not the

best person for this," he admitted. "Maybe you should have invited Chloe instead."

Zee lifted a hanger off the rod, then looked at Jasper seriously. "I'm not sure I can trust Chloe."

"Why not?" Jasper asked, shocked. "She always wears nice clothes."

"That's not what I mean." Zee took a deep breath. "I think she may have taken my diary."

"Why would she do it?" Jasper said.

"I don't know, but all the proof says she did." She listed the evidence that pointed right at Chloe.

Jasper was silent for a moment. Then he shook his head. "Something's not right. She barely even knew you when your diary disappeared. I'm sure we'll figure out Chloe couldn't have done it. And we'll find out who did."

"I hope so," Zee said. She held up a pink silk dress. "What do you think?"

Jasper studied it and nodded. "Cool."

Zee slipped behind a screen and pulled the dress on. The flowing sleeves looked like little angel wings. One of them hung down off her shoulder. She went to show her dad.

"Wow, Zee!" Mr. Carmichael beamed. "You look like a star! I like it."

Zee stared at herself in the mirror and had to admit—of

all the dresses she'd tried on—it was the best one.

With her new dress in hand, Zee practically skipped down the long hallway toward the elevators. Jasper and her father walked ahead, and Jasper started to recommend energy-saving lightbulbs.

Blown-up magazine covers hung in frames along the walls. Zee had passed them a million times and never paid much attention, but today she wanted to see if her dress was featured on a cover. Suddenly she stopped cold and stared. The cover headline read, "The 25 Best Bands You Don't Know." Underneath, a familiar face stared back at Zee. She moved a little closer, then stepped back again.

"Dad!" Zee called out. "Who are these guys?"

Mr. Carmichael stopped midstride and turned around. "Oh, that's Yes No. They were a big success in Europe."

"I've never heard of them," Jasper said. He walked over to Zee.

"That was about ten years ago," Mr. Carmichael explained. "Then they sort of fizzled out."

"Do you see who I see?" Zee asked her friend.

Jasper turned to look at her with wide eyes. "Mr. P was in Yes No."

"I can't believe it," Zee groaned. "I humiliated an international singing sensation!"

Hi, Diary,

I can't take it anymore!!! I have to know who took my diary—and who has been sending me creepy messages. Jasper's going to help me work on the mystery during study hall today, but I don't think I can wait until then. It might be too late. If Chloe is the thief, she might spring "The Big Surprise" on me by then. It makes sense to confront her. I've done the calculations. Check them out here

The Worst That Can Happen
1. I'm wrong about Chloe, and we can be friends again.

The Best That Can Happen
1. I find out who stole my diary.
2. I avoid The Big Surprise.
3. I don't suffer any more public humiliation.
4. I'm wrong about Chloe, and we can be friends again. ☺

See? It makes sense. It can't hurt to ask.

Zee

Still, Zee hardly ever made such a big decision without Ally's advice.

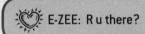

E-ZEE: R u there?

Ally wasn't. Zee would just have to figure out what to do on her own.

As Zee walked across the Brookdale campus, her Sidekick buzzed. A text message from Landon!

>Can u stay after school 2day?

>Sure. Y?

>I might try out 4 teen sing and need help.

Landon had actually meant it when he had said he wanted her help! As Zee went inside the building, she was glad he hadn't asked her in person. Her heart was pounding so loudly, she was sure anyone within ten feet could hear it.

Inside, Zee peered around the corner just enough to see Chloe at her locker placing her books on the top shelf. Zee watched Chloe hang her bag on a hook and shut the door.

Zee prepared for her next move. She had practiced talking to Chloe all night long. (Who needs sleep?) She figured she could make a how-to DVD called, *Keeping It Friendly: How to Accuse Someone of Stealing Your Most Private Thoughts*. She was just going to go up to Chloe and say, *This probably sounds weird, but I was wondering if maybe you got my diary by mistake*. Chloe could just say, *Yeah, isn't that bizarre? I have no idea how it ended up in my bag*. Zee would get her diary back, and Chloe could keep her pride.

As Zee waited for the coast to be completely clear, she could hardly believe what she saw. With her music folder in hand, Chloe shut her locker, picked up her cello, and just walked away. She didn't put the lock back on. The locker might as well have been wide open, screaming, "Please, Zee, look inside!" Cool beans! Zee could just take the diary and save Chloe a ton of embarrassment. In fact, maybe that's *exactly* what Chloe wanted her to do. Maybe that's why she didn't lock it.

Dodging sleepy upperclassmen with hot cups of coffee and a trio of ninth graders walking and texting at the same time, Zee wove her way to Chloe's locker. Zee took a quick look to the left, then to the right. All clear! She pulled up the handle and casually popped the door open. She carefully flipped through the math, Spanish, and science textbooks on the top shelf. No diary. Slowly Zee reached for Chloe's bag, lifted the flap, and reached in. *Ohmylanta!* Zee thought as her hand clasped a small book. The diary! *I was right!*

Her heart pounding, Zee pulled the book out of the bag.

"What are you doing?" a voice behind her asked. A voice with a Southern accent.

Zee spun around. "I wanted to get *this*," she said, holding the book for Chloe to see.

Chloe looked confused. "The novel we're reading for English?" Zee looked down. It wasn't her diary at all. "You were snooping in my locker."

Yup. That's what Zee was doing—which made it hard to figure out what to say next. "Ummm . . . ," she stalled.

"Why would you do that?" Chloe asked.

Zee's shoulders slumped. "I thought maybe you took my diary."

"Huh? You're my friend." Chloe's twang caught on the lump that was forming in her throat.

Zee wanted to believe her, but her thoughts were all mixed up. "You were the only one in the music room when that note was written on the board."

"I wasn't even *in* the room," Chloe defended herself. "I didn't want to hang out all by myself, so I went to the bathroom while you checked the lost and found. I got back right before you did."

"What about when you went upstairs in my house before Marcus's party?" Zee asked. "Did you even go to the bathroom?"

"No," Chloe said quietly, looking down. "I wanted to see what Adam's room looked like. When I heard you coming upstairs, I panicked. I shut his door and ran into your room." When Chloe looked up again, Zee could see that she was blushing. "I know I shouldn't have been snooping around, but I didn't *steal* anything." She shut her locker door, then put the lock on, making sure it was secure. "I didn't even go into his room."

As Chloe stormed off, Zee leaned against the locker and slid down to the floor.

Student Teacher

Hi, Diary,

Wow! The first-period bell hasn't even rung, and I've already lost a friend. ☹ ☹

How could I have messed up sooooo badly?!?! Chloe's not a thief at all—she has a crush on Adam. Bleh! I have no idea how that's even possible. I mean, he's nice and all, but she saw his room. It's disgusting. (Hang up your clothes and throw away your takeout containers.) YUCK!!! I _do_ _not_ get it.

Still, I feel awful. And I don't know how to fix it.

Zee

Chloe wasn't Zee's only problem. As she stepped through the door to music class, giant purple letters on the whiteboard screamed,

I WONDER IF LANDON WILL BE CUTER
THIS YEAR THAN HE WAS LAST YEAR
—MACKENZIE BLUE

Zee looked at Chloe, but she couldn't read her expression. She rushed to the front of the room and, with a shaky hand, picked up an eraser and furiously removed every last piece of evidence. To her horror, she had to pass Landon to get to her seat. She gave him an apologetic half smile, but a bright shade of red had replaced his tan. He was as embarrassed as she was and couldn't even look at her.

Of course, Zee had had such a busy morning upsetting people, she'd practically forgotten all about what she, Kathi, and Jen had done to Mr. P Friday night. Until the bell rang and he came in the room. Ugh!

Mr. P tapped his baton on his desk. "Settle down, everyone!" he called over the murmurs and giggles that were still bouncing around the room. Gradually the noise died to a silence. "We're going to try something different today."

Zee sat at attention. Something different was exactly what she needed.

"One day each week," Mr. P continued, "I'm going to select a different student to lead the class. Once you understand how we make music as a group, you'll be stronger individual musicians."

Marcus raised his hand and asked, "Do we get to pick the music we play? Because I have a set that I think would sound great."

"No." Mr. P laughed. "I'll pick the music, and I'll be right next to you to give you tips. But you'll mark the beat and help me keep the group on track."

Kathi sighed so loudly, they must have heard it all the way in the main office. Then she leaned toward Jen. "I guess he knows his students are better teachers than he is," she whispered so everyone could hear.

Suddenly it was clear to Zee. Kathi hadn't gone to Mr. P's concert to hear his music. She'd gone to humiliate him—and she'd used Zee to help do it. She couldn't believe she had actually fallen for the popular girl's phony-friend act. Although she didn't think it was possible, Zee felt even more awful. It was time for a new list. This one would have to be in her head.

Ways My Life Could Get Worse

1. *Walk around with a booger hanging out of my nose.*
2. *Body slam the head of school on my way to second period.*
3.

"Our first student leader will be Mackenzie Carmichael."

Yes, that would definitely make my life worse. Wait! Zee hadn't thought that! Someone had said it. She looked at Mr. P. *Oh no.* He was smiling right at her.

"Mackenzie, come on up here," Mr. P suggested, gesturing toward the front of the room.

Before she got up, Zee gazed down at herself. In her worst dreams, she showed up at school wearing a bra on the outside of her blouse. Luckily she had on her shirt and vest, shortened skirt, monkey-head socks, and her new chocolate Converse All Star sneakers. What a relief!

Zee rose up out of her seat and walked to the front of the silent room. Mr. P handed Zee his baton. Zee took it and turned to the class. Now what would she do? She was too embarrassed to look at her classmates.

Evidently eye contact was an important requirement

for leading a group of musicians. Mr. P's experiment was a disaster. Landon's drums were way out of sync. Chloe kept losing focus. Jasper didn't know whether to follow Mr. P or Zee on his bass. Even perfect Kathi was off. As usual, Jen followed Kathi, and it sounded as though she was purposely hitting her wooden marimba bars off beat. Marcus followed Mr. P's downbeat on his piano, but it wasn't enough to save the group. They must have stopped and started again a hundred times, but each version was worse than the one before.

"Great job, everyone!" Mr. P announced at the end of the period. *Really?* Zee thought. *How is that even possible?* As she handed the baton back to her teacher, it didn't take long for her to figure out why Mr. P was so happy. Of course! He had chosen her to lead the group to punish her for Friday night. He was angry that she had humiliated him at the concert—especially after he had helped her out with her *Teen Sing* audition. And now he had gotten her back.

Outside in the hallway, Jasper and Chloe were standing with their heads together. Zee couldn't hear what they were talking about, but when Chloe saw her coming, she turned and went off toward English class without waiting for Zee.

Zee pasted on a smile and walked up to Jasper. "So, are you going to help me crack 'The Case of the Missing Diary' during study hall?" she said, even though she really wanted to ask, *Are you still my friend?* Chloe must have told him what had happened.

Jasper slapped himself on the forehead. "Oh, bother! I forgot. I'm really sorry, Zee," he apologized. "Chloe and I need to work on our science project."

"Oh, okay," Zee said, wondering if that was his polite British way of telling her he didn't want to be friends anymore.

Landon zipped past Zee—without saying hello or good-bye. *I guess he doesn't want my help for* Teen Sing *now*, she thought. And since Mr. P was obviously angry with her, Zee decided to go home right after school instead of practicing with him, too.

In study hall, Zee sat at a desk in the corner, as far away from everyone else as was humanly possible. She pulled out a piece of paper and began writing.

> Hi, Diary,
>   Jasper's choosing Chloe over me. Who can blame him? I wasn't a very good friend to Chloe. I mean

"Hi, Zee," Kathi interrupted her. Zee slipped the sheet of paper into her binder as Kathi and Jen sat down next to her.

"Hi." Zee wanted to tell Kathi that she didn't appreciate being tricked into going to see The Crew. But at that moment, she didn't feel like having another embarrassing confrontation.

Kathi had something else on her mind anyway. She stuck her lip out to make a major pouty face. "Couldn't you just die? That note on the board was the *worst*."

"Yeah," Zee said weakly, not wanting to talk about it.

Jen looked over at Jasper and Chloe, who were sitting in front of a computer. Jasper was typing on the keyboard while Chloe pointed to something on the screen. "Boy, they got chummy really fast," Jen said.

Zee pretended not to care. "They have to work on their science project together."

"What is it about anyway?" Kathi asked.

"I don't know. They want to keep it a secret."

"A secret?" Kathi looked stunned. "From their best friend?"

Zee shrugged. "That's okay." No matter what she said to Kathi, though, she couldn't hide her fears from herself. Maybe they never really were friends. What if Jasper never cared about Zee and was just waiting for someone better to come along?

Then Zee realized that talking to Kathi had actually helped. "The science project!" Zee said out loud, remembering something important. She had left Jasper alone with her bag the day he came over to borrow the book. The day the diary was stolen.

"What about it?" Jen asked.

"Oh, nothing," Zee said. But she knew it was much more than nothing. It was huge! If Jasper wasn't the friend she thought he was, maybe he was the kind of person who would steal her diary.

13

Detective Disaster

By the time Zee had walked into her house that after-
noon, she was greeted by a miracle—and her mother.

"Hi, honey," Mrs. Carmichael said. "I thought you were
staying after school to work on your *Teen Sing* song."

Zee opened the snack cabinet and peered inside for the
perfect I-had-a-bad-day treat. "Uhhh, change of plans. I'm
taking the day off."

"Well, I'm going over to help Jasper's mother. She's starting her party-planning business, and I promised to give her
the lowdown on Brookdale since she doesn't know the area
very well yet. You know, the best caterers, halls, and florists.
Want to come?"

Does a dog bark?

Zee had watched and studied Jasper until the end of study hall. After what had happened with Chloe, she knew she had to be careful about investigating him. She overheard the two of them talking about putting the final touches on their science project model—at Chloe's house.

Zee's mother had no idea Jasper wouldn't be home. It was the perfect opportunity.

"Sure," Zee told her mother, grabbing a bag of cheddar cheese popcorn from the shelf.

"I'm sorry, Mackenzie," Mrs. Chapman said in a British accent. She was a tall woman who always wore her long brown hair twisted up on the back of her head. She was really nice, but she always seemed a little nervous. "Jasper's not here."

Zee made her most convincing disappointed face. "Darn!" she said. "Jasper borrowed a book from me a few weeks ago. Do you think it would be okay if I look for it?"

"Why don't you ring him up and see if he knows where it is?" Jasper's mom said.

"No!" Zee practically shouted. Mrs. Chapman flinched at the outburst. "I mean, I wouldn't want to bother him."

Luckily that was all Jasper's mother had to hear. She nodded and said, "It's likely on his bookcase or right on top of his desk anyway." She turned to Mrs. Carmichael and laughed. "He's more organized than I am."

Taking the steps two at a time, Zee hurried into Jasper's bedroom. *Everything* was in place. It was immaculate! She checked the most obvious places—the bookcase, the desk, the nightstand. But she knew Jasper was way too smart to leave her diary out in the open.

Zee sat in Jasper's desk chair and pulled open the center drawer. Wow! Pencils were neatly lined up in a long plastic box. Pens were in another. Other little boxes held paper clips, erasers, and thumbtacks. Zee's desk drawer was reserved for

all the stuff she could never throw out but would never—ever—use again. When she needed a pencil, she just yelled, "Mom, where's a pencil?"

At least Jasper's system made it easy to see that there was no diary. Zee bent over and pulled open the other drawers. File folders with labels TESTS, EXTRA PAPER, and REPORT CARDS hung side by side. Zee placed her hand near the back of the drawer, looking for a tab that said, ZEE'S DIARY. But there was no folder with that label and no diary in the others.

Zee looked around the room. *The closet!* She opened the doors and looked inside. She knew she had to work quickly and put the neatly stacked containers back *exactly* the way she'd found them. She'd clean up the mess she made on the desk afterward. On her hands and knees, she removed the lid to a photo box. Mostly there were baby photos of Jasper. Playing in the sand. Smearing spaghetti in his hair. Riding his tricycle. She pulled the stack out to get to the bottom. That's when she saw it—a picture of Jasper and her at the pool. Posed with their arms around each other, they were licking mint chocolate chip ice cream, their favorite flavor. She and Jasper may have been different in a lot of ways, but they had the most important thing in common—they were great friends. Zee's suspicions melted

away like those ice cream cones had on that hot day. A familiar, unpleasant feeling—guilt—replaced them.

Before Zee could put the lid on the box and shut the closet door, she heard a sound in the hall. When she turned around, the two mothers were staring at her—Mrs. Chapman looked confused and Mrs. Carmichael looked angry. They had caught Zee red-handed!

The keys clattered as Mrs. Carmichael tossed them on the black granite kitchen counter. But the noise couldn't cover her words. "What were you *thinking*? Thanks to the fact that you were rummaging through Jasper's room, I didn't even get to help Lucy with her business."

Mrs. Carmichael hardly ever got this upset, and Zee knew what she had done was wrong. Really wrong. But she had to admit that her mother's lecture was a hundred times better than Mrs. Chapman's hurt silence.

Zee thought—and silently pleaded—that her mother might stop when Adam arrived after tennis practice. No such luck.

Adam pulled up a chair as if he were watching his favorite TV show. "I wonder how you would feel if Jasper went through your most personal belongings," Mrs. Carmichael continued.

"But I thought he had *read* my most personal thoughts," Zee defended herself. "I thought he took my diary."

"Did he?"

"Well . . . no."

Mrs. Carmichael planted her hand on her hip, waiting for Zee to say more.

"May I go to my room?" Zee asked.

"I think that's a good idea," her mother told her. When Zee got upstairs, she threw herself facedown on her bed and buried her head in a pillow. She knew Jasper would be upset when Mrs. Chapman told him what she had done.

Knock. Knock. "Can I come in?" Adam had followed her upstairs.

"Yes." At least someone still wanted to talk to her.

"Hi," Adam said, trying to be both serious and cheerful. "I heard about what was on the music room board today." He sat on the edge of the bed next to her.

"Excellent," Zee sighed. "Now the whole school knows what I wrote in my diary."

"Did you really think Jasper could do that to you?"

Zee hung her head. "I guess not," she said quietly. "But I need to stop whoever took my diary."

"Maybe you need to get a grip."

Oh, great, Zee thought. *Now my brother gets to lecture me.*

"I've never read your diary," Adam continued, "but I know you have a crush on Landon."

"You do?"

"You go all mushy and googly eyed every time someone mentions his name."

"But those were the *exact* words in my diary. My most private thoughts." The sick feeling returned to Zee's stomach.

Adam shook his head. "You're not getting it. The point isn't that someone took your diary or that you have a crush on Landon. From what I hear, so do half of the seventh-grade girls."

Zee sat up. "So what *is* the point?" She definitely wasn't getting it.

"You don't have as many secrets as you think. Nobody does. We're all open books in a lot of ways."

"Really?"

"Sure. You can tell a lot about people just by looking at them. Like the way we know when Dad has landed an exclusive celebrity interview that he can't talk about."

"He whistles."

"Exactly!" Adam said.

"And the way girls make Jasper so nervous." Zee laughed. "It's written all over his face."

Adam stood up and looked at Zee. "Someone is being mean, but you don't have to let them get to you."

"I don't know . . . " Zee said, still unsure.

"Just have confidence and don't apologize for who you are. Because you may not be perfect, but you are a pretty awesome sister."

"You think so?"

Adam nodded and turned to go. "But don't spread that around."

"Your secret's safe with me!" Zee called as he walked out.

Adam had definitely made Zee feel better, but—unless you counted Kathi and Jen—she still didn't have any friends. Except Ally.

E-ZEE: R u still talking 2 me.

 SPARKLEGRRL: Of course! Y?

Zee filled her best friend in on everything that had happened that day.

 SPARKLEGRRL: It's a good thing u want 2 b a singer and not a detective.

 E-ZEE: LOL!

 SPARKLEGRRL: Don't worry, Z. U will find a way 2 fix this.

 E-ZEE: How was the party?

 SPARKLEGRRL: AWFUL! I wore the high heels—and fell on my butt. Down the stairs.

 E-ZEE: Oh no!

SPARKLEGRRL: My dress got caught on the railing, and every1 could c the RIDICULOUS bra my mother made me wear!

 E-ZEE: U need a bra?

 SPARKLEGRRL: NO! She's just being weird.

 E-ZEE: Yeah—I understand.

Zee felt incredibly bad for Ally, but after all that had happened that day, it was great to have a friend whom Zee trusted so much—and who trusted her.

 SPARKLEGRRL: What's up w Teen Sing?

 E-ZEE: Now that Mr. P is mad @ me, I don't know if I'll b ready. There's a rehearsal this week.

SPARKLEGRRL: You'd better get used 2 every1 knowing ur secrets. That's what it will b like when ur a famous pop star. Zee on the cover of Star mag!

But Zee didn't bother to play along. Her dreams of becoming a star seemed as far away as her best friend.

The Diary Thief

How to Make Sure You Have No Friends

1. Accuse them of stealing your diary. That should do it. It worked for me.

Jasper and Chloe presented their science project that Wednesday.

"It took a lot of people and money to turn Brookdale Academy into a green school," Jasper began.

"But there are lots of environmentally friendly things students and staff can do to help the Earth," Chloe continued.

Jasper and Chloe revealed their secret plan how Brookdale Academy could do more to become even greener. They showed how easy it would be for students and teachers to begin composting paper, leaves, and cafeteria scraps.

"The compost can go into garden beds around campus, and students can tend the gardens," Jasper said. He pointed to a miniature model of Brookdale Academy. Tiny gardens dotted the lawn. "One day, we might grow the vegetables that end up on the lunch tray."

Jen actually got excited about the idea. "From the cafeteria to the garden and back to the cafeteria," she summarized.

"Precisely," Jasper said, pleased that other students were interested. "It's a brilliant plan, really!" Then he blushed and said, "I mean, it would be a good idea."

Chloe talked about how important animals were to growing plants. "Putting worms in compost bins really speeds up the process, and manure is full of nutrients for the soil," she explained.

Jen's enthusiasm disappeared. "Nasty!" she protested. "I think I'll just get my food from the grocery store."

Jasper and Chloe's PowerPoint presentation included charts and drawings. When an illustration of hungry worms wearing school uniforms and munching on leaves appeared on the screen, the whole class laughed.

Zee was really impressed and decided to tell Jasper and Chloe—even though now neither one of them was speaking to her.

As soon as the bell rang, Zee went right up to Chloe. "Wow! That was a great presentation," Zee told her, trying to sound casual but enthusiastic.

"Thanks," Chloe said politely.

Chloe had actually answered Zee! Filled with hope, Zee went on, "I mean, I had no idea how important compost was until today."

"Good to know," Jasper responded.

"If you want to—"

"I have to go," Chloe said, breaking away and moving toward the door.

Jasper followed. "Me, too," he said and left Zee standing by herself.

With her shirt hanging out of her uniform skirt and her hair going every which way, Zee stumbled downstairs to the kitchen the next morning. She hadn't had time to put herself completely together yet, but she wanted to ask her father to drop her off early at school. She'd fix herself in the SUV on the way there.

"Whoa!" Adam said. "Did you have a run-in with the undead last night, Bride of Frankenstein?"

Zee poured herself a glass of orange juice. "Funny stuff," she said, but she had to admit she wasn't exactly thrilled about the way she looked—or felt—either. She had tossed and turned all night long. She'd finally fallen asleep, but by then she was so exhausted, she didn't hear her alarm go off a few hours later.

"Were you worried about the *Teen Sing* rehearsal, honey?" Mrs. Carmichael asked.

Zee nodded as she took a gulp of her drink. It would

have been bad enough to have to sing in front of the entire school. Or to have her friends mad at her. But Zee had both problems. At least her mother had forgiven her.

"You'll feel better once you've performed your song today," Mrs. Carmichael said, placing a bowl on the table. "Have some oatmeal."

"No thanks, Mom," Zee said. She grabbed a breakfast bar from the cabinet and shoved it into her book bag. "I'm going to get a ride with Dad today. I need to get to school as early as I can." She had decided to talk to the only person she knew who could understand how she was feeling—Mr. P. Zee was sure he had had to perform even when he didn't feel like it.

Mrs. Carmichael handed Zee a banana. "You need your energy."

"Thanks, Mom," Zee said, taking the fruit and sprinting out of the kitchen. "I've gotta go tell Dad to hurry up."

As Zee approached the music room, she wondered if Mr. P would be willing to help her after what had happened at the concert. She'd soon find out. She was just steps away from the room—close enough to hear her teacher's voice. "I underst—," he said. There was a long pause. "I think th—." Mr. P was on the phone, and whoever was on the other end kept interrupting him. Zee leaned against the wall outside and listened. There was a long silence, and for a minute Zee thought that maybe Mr. P had ended his phone call, until he finally said, "Yes, I know Mrs. Bradley was a wonderful teacher, but we all have different styles." Another pause. "Yes, I think I *do* have a style."

He must be talking to someone's parent! Zee thought. *I bet it's Kathi's.* She was always complaining.

One thing was certain—this was not a good time to ask for help. Zee would have to solve her problem on her own.

* * *

Zee's *Teen Sing* rehearsal was at 4:25. That gave her time to change into the clothes she'd picked out especially for the occasion—a navy blue halter dress with a black camisole underneath. (It was hard to feel like a star in a school uniform.) And she would still have time to warm up. By the time she got to the auditorium, the room was full of *Teen Sing* competitors, their fan clubs, and other curious students. A microphone in one hand, Marcus gave her a thumbs-up with the other one. He was part of the stage crew.

Jasper and Chloe sat together in a corner of the room. If they saw Zee, they didn't let on. As much as she wanted to talk to them, it was obvious they didn't feel the same way. She had her rehearsal to think about anyway. She pulled out her guitar and began tuning it—just as the next act began to sing.

It was a familiar voice. Kathi's. "'*Jump in the water—it's cooler, baby. Dive in the water—it's better, baby.*'" And a familiar song! Zee's! Kathi was singing the song Zee had written in her diary. The tune was different, but the words were definitely hers. Zee had never sung that song for anyone except Mr. P and Chloe.

Kathi had stolen Zee's diary! Zee raced over to the stage stairs. She could see Jen waiting backstage.

When Kathi was done performing, hoots, cheers, and applause roared through the auditorium. As she left the stage, she waved and blew kisses to the crowd. "You sounded soooooo great!" Jen gushed. Neither girl noticed Zee—until Kathi bumped right into her.

At first, Kathi looked stunned, then she started laughing. "Did you like my *big surprise*?" she asked.

"Not really—since it was my song!" Zee growled between clenched teeth.

"Congratulations, Detective Obvious," Kathi taunted. "Unfortunately you don't have any evidence."

"Mr. P and Chloe heard me sing it."

Kathi rolled her eyes. "Yeah, I don't think a substitute teacher wants to go up against my family with the head of school, do you?" She paused to let her words sink in. "And as for Chloe, do you really think she'll want to stick up for you?" She didn't wait for a response. "Without the diary, you'll never be able to prove you wrote the song."

"But you *took* my diary."

"*Technically* I didn't take it. Someone might have given it to me though." Kathi slowly turned to Jen, then grabbed her friend and walked off. Jen couldn't look at Zee. Instead she guiltily turned her eyes to the ground.

Zee was confused. Had Jen taken her diary? When? That first day, they had been together—in French and science— but Zee hadn't left Jen with her bag.

With a sinking feeling in her heart, Zee watched Kathi and Jen meet Landon across the auditorium. He handed Kathi her book bag.

"That's it!" Zee shouted, then immediately slapped her hand across her mouth. Everything had spilled out of her book bag the first day of school when she'd bumped into Landon. Jen must have picked up the diary—and kept it!

"Mackenzie Carmichael!" a woman shouted from the stage. "You're up next!"

What should she do? No matter how well Zee sang, it would look like she was the one who stole Kathi's song.

"Mackenzie Carmichael!" the voice called out again.

"Ummmm . . ." Mackenzie called up to the woman. "I'm good. I don't need to rehearse."

"Are you sure? You won't get another chance until the real deal."

Zee nodded. "I'm sure."

Only she wasn't. *Ohmylanta!* She had to figure out what to do. Of course, she was going to need Ally's help.

 E-ZEE: I can't believe I trusted Kathi and Jen.

At home that night, Zee told Ally all about what had happened that day, then waited for Ally's reply. She wouldn't have blamed her if she had said, "I told you so."

 SPARKLEGRRL: Every1 makes mistakes. U just want 2 have friends.

E-ZEE: So how did I end up w NO friends?

 SPARKLEGRRL: I'm ur friend. ☺

 E-ZEE: BFF!!! But I don't think Jasper and
Chloe will ever want 2 b my friends again.

 SPARKLEGRRL: Don't b so sure.
Think about all the little
fights we've had. All we had 2
do was say, "I'm sorry," and
everything was OK.

 E-ZEE: OMG!!!!

 SPARKLEGRRL: What??!!

 E-ZEE: I never said I was sorry 4 accusing them.

 SPARKLEGRRL: U should.

 E-ZEE: I will!!! But 1st tell me what ur mother
did when she found out u wore those high heels.

SPARKLEGRRL: Nothing. She said my sore butt was probably a good enuf reason 4 me NOT to do it again.

 E-ZEE: LOL!

 SPARKLEGRRL: And I met a boy. He says he likes my trés Americaine look—even my sneakers! We're going 2 go 2 the Eiffel Tower—très touristy—and get pizza. It's his favorite American food. Mine 2!

Before Zee could shut down her computer for the night, she had an email to write.

Hi, Chloe and Jasper,

I know I'm probably the last person you want to talk to right now, but I need to tell you that I'm sorry. I know you would never take my diary. I kind of went crazy and wasn't thinking. You are great

friends. And even though I wouldn't blame you
if you never spoke to me again, I hope you will.
(Please.)

☺ Zee

Then she turned out the lights and crawled into bed.

15

The Apology

The next morning, Zee had another apology to make. She headed straight for the music room.

It was still pretty early, so Mr. P was alone in the room. But he barely looked like the eager new teacher from the first day. Or the cool international rock-and-roll star from his concert. Dark circles hung under his eyes. His hair was sticking up all over the place. And his shirt was misbuttoned. Mr. P must have felt as bad as he looked. He was sitting at his desk with his head in his hands.

"I'm sorry," Zee blurted out.

Mr. P looked up. "For what?"

"I didn't mean to embarrass you at your concert."

Mr. P looked confused. "You didn't embarrass me.

Actually I was very happy to see some friendly faces. The whole night was outrageously nerve-racking."

Zee wasn't going to let herself off that easy. "Maybe we shouldn't have brought up that you're a teacher—you know, since you used to be such a big rock star."

Mr. P laughed, stood up, and crossed his arms over his chest. "Well, I'd say I was a *medium* rock star." He paused and looked at Zee. "But it was my choice to leave. All the touring and recording just weren't fun anymore. When work isn't fun, it's time to try something new. And being a teacher is something I've always wanted to do."

Zee examined his exhausted expression and wondered if it was still something he wanted to do. "Is teaching fun?" she asked carefully.

Mr. P's face lit up for the first time all morning. "Teaching *is* fun, but . . . challenging . . . sometimes." His smile disappeared as he said, "I hope I can meet those challenges— before it's too late."

"Too late for what?" Zee asked.

Mr. P sighed. "It's just an expression." Then he perked up a little again. "How did rehearsal go yesterday?"

"Ohmylanta!" Zee said. She'd been so focused on

apologizing to Mr. P, she'd forgotten about her song crisis.

"What?"

"It's just an expression, too," Zee said, shrugging. Then she told Mr. P that her diary and song were stolen. She didn't mention Kathi's name. He'd figure it out when he heard Kathi sing. "Since I don't have a song, I may not audition for *Teen Sing* after all."

"You're just going to quit?" When Mr. P put it that way, it sounded so awful. Zee's teacher laid a hand on her shoulder and looked at her seriously. "At some point, you have to stand up to those people."

"Did anything like this ever happen to you?" Zee asked.

Mr. P nodded. "The first professional band I was in, one of the other guys got a solo deal and stole my song."

"What did you do?"

"After I finished yelling at him and calling him names, there was nothing I could do. Then I realized that only musicians who are afraid they don't have talent steal from other people."

"He wasn't talented?"

"He was. But he wasn't cut out to be a soloist." Mr. P gave a sly smile. "Of course, it made me kind of happy that that song was the only hit he ever had."

Zee thought about what Mr. P had told her. "I'm still

not sure what to do about *Teen Sing*."

"Pick a new song. There are lots of them out there."

"But I want to write my own. I want to be a singer *and* a songwriter. I want to stand out."

"So do it." He moved over to the piano and sat down on the bench. "What have you been working on?"

Zee followed her teacher across the room. "It's a song about my favorite nail polish—Miami Sunset. But I'm stuck on a rhyme for *orange*."

"I see." Thinking, Mr. P moved his lips from side to side. He laid his fingers on the piano keys. "It's great to write about what you know, but it's really cool when you take a risk and are honest about your feelings."

"I'm so scared of being honest," Zee sighed. "I'm tired of having everyone know my secrets."

Mr. P played the piano and sang, *"I'm so scared of being honest, so tired of all my secrets."*

Zee's eyes grew wide. "Did you just write that?"

Mr. P smiled. "No, you did. Write the next line."

Zee took a deep breath. *"There's a place I used to put them, all the things I was afraid of,"* she sang as Mr. P joined in on the piano. She opened her eyes and smiled. "You're a really good teacher!"

"Thanks!"

16

True Friends

As soon as class began, Mr. P called Jasper up to be class leader. With a serious expression on his face, Jasper stood very straight and tapped the beat on a music stand with his baton.

The group was starting to sound better, and Zee played along, but she could barely focus on the music. Had Chloe and Jasper gotten her email? Did they want to be friends? Zee couldn't tell.

When the bell finally rang, Jasper and Chloe gathered their instruments and books and left without Zee. *I guess they really don't like me anymore,* Zee thought. *Maybe we won't ever be friends again.*

✳ ✳ ✳

When Zee walked into French class, Jen and Marcus were already there talking to each other.

" . . . and my brother said, 'Next time you burn a CD for me, could you include at least *one* band I've actually heard of?'" Marcus finished. Jen threw her head back and laughed way too hard. Zee hated the thought of having to sit right next to phony Jen, but Madame Frazier had assigned seating.

Zee slid into her chair and looked straight ahead. "Hi, Zee," Marcus said.

"Hi, Marcus," she answered, still avoiding Jen's glance.

Marcus looked from one girl to the other. "Is there something going on I don't know about?" he asked.

Jen said to Marcus, "Kinda. Can I talk to Zee in private for a sec?"

"I'm not even here," Marcus said, turning around and sticking an index finger in each ear. *"La la la la la."*

Jen swiveled in her seat so that she was facing Zee. Not wanting to give her the satisfaction of her full attention, Zee turned slightly in Jen's direction. "I'm really sorry, Zee," Jen apologized. "I thought Kathi was just going to read your diary. I didn't know she was going to use it against you like that."

"But it was *mine*," Zee said. "It was nobody else's business."

"I know," Jen replied, "and I feel awful about what I did.

I made a huge mistake."

A mistake. Jen's words echoed in Zee's head. She knew all about mistakes. All she wanted was an apology. How could she expect Chloe and Jasper to forgive her if she didn't accept Jen's? "It's okay," she said. And she meant it.

Zee looked up and down the seventh-grade lunch tables, searching for a place to sit. Since they'd stopped talking to Zee, Jasper and Chloe had avoided her by eating at a different table from the rest of the music class gang. And now there was no way Zee could sit by Kathi, so she'd have to eat somewhere else, too.

Jen approached with her lunch tray. Good. Maybe she and Jen could sit together. "Hi," Zee called out to her.

With Kathi watching from her lunch spot, Jen quietly whispered, "Hi," without even bothering to look at Zee.

Unbelievable! Zee thought. Jen might have been sorry, but she was still under Kathi's spell.

Zee was stuck. Doomed to eat lunch all by herself for the rest of the year, she took the closest seat. As she unzipped her lunchbox, her Sidekick buzzed. A text message read,

>Want 2 sit w us?

Zee looked over at Chloe and Jasper, who were smiling at her.

"Your project was just so awesome!" Zee said as the three friends walked down the sun-filled halls toward science together. She had so much to tell them, she was practically bursting. "You won't believe what Kathi's parents are doing to Mr. P. I think they're trying to get him fired."

"Really?" Jasper said.

"I mean, if it weren't for him, I wouldn't even be auditioning for *Teen Sing*," Zee continued. Their conversation was interrupted by loud voices coming out of the head of school's office.

"We chose this school for our daughter because of the excellent music program." A woman's voice drifted through the closed door to the hall. "They haven't seen a note of classical music. This Mr. . . . P . . . doesn't know what he's doing. If you don't fix the problem, we will have to consider withdrawing her—and we'll expect our tuition back."

Then the head of school's door flew open. A tall woman in a dark gray business suit passed through it, then suddenly stopped when she saw Chloe. "Hi, honey," she said in a smooth Southern accent. She smiled warmly.

Chloe looked from the woman to Zee and back to the

woman. "Hi, Mom," she answered awkwardly.

Ohmylanta! Zee thought. *That isn't Kathi's mother! It's Chloe's.* Now Zee understood why Chloe couldn't go to the amphitheater and couldn't audition for *Teen Sing.* Her parents didn't approve of Mr. P.

"Mom, this is my friend Zee," Chloe said.

Mrs. Lawrence-Johnson smiled at Zee. "I'm so happy to meet you." Zee wanted to be angry with Chloe's mother. After all, she was trying to get her favorite teacher fired. But she couldn't ignore this other, kinder side of Mrs. Lawrence-Johnson. Especially when she rubbed her hands together and asked, "Who wants to go to Wink! after school? I just won my case this morning, and I'm dying to celebrate."

Mrs. Lawrence-Johnson had said the magic word. Wink! was Zee's favorite spa. She never turned down a chance to go there.

"Cool beans!" Zee said. "I'm in."

"Are you coming?" Chloe asked Jasper.

Jasper looked at the six eyes fixed on him like a lamb surrounded by wolves. "No, thank you," he said carefully. "I think I'd feel rather strange getting my nails done."

The three friends giggled, but Zee laughed the hardest, happy to be together again with her new, true friends.

Dear Diary,

Was I jealous of Chloe and Jasper? Is that why I totally lost my mind and accused them of stealing my diary? (Answer key: Yes!) I just didn't realize it. My whole life it has always been just Zee and Ally. I never really had to share my best friend with anyone. Now it's the three of us. I may be in upper school, but I guess I could still use a few lessons in sharing.

Zee

* * *

"I can't really blame you for suspecting me," Chloe said. She was sitting under the dryer in the chair next to Zee, their hair wrapped. "I *was* hiding something from you. You liked Mr. P so much, and I was afraid you wouldn't like me if you knew how my parents felt about him and *Teen Sing*."

Zee thought back to the first day of school, when she had made her father drop her off a block from school because she had been so embarrassed by his SUV. "Let's make a pact," she suggested, "that we won't freak out about the things our parents do."

"It's a deal," Chloe said, holding up her right hand. Zee high-fived it.

"Oh. My. Gosh!" Chloe mouthed, pointing to the salon's entrance. Kathi had just walked in. The girls froze as Kathi passed by on her way to the spray-tanning booths. But with their heads wrapped—and Kathi's nose high in the air, as usual—she didn't even recognize them.

"Are you thinking what I'm thinking?" Zee asked.

"Revenge!" Chloe said excitedly.

They watched as Kathi stepped inside the booth. The spa employee told her, "Get ready, and I'll be right back to apply your bronzer." Then she shut the door, adjusted some controls, and walked away.

In the next second, Zee and Chloe were outside the
booth door. They looked at the controls, which were set to
"summer light."

Chloe pointed to the highest setting on the knob—
"super dark." "Kathi will be as orange as a carrot," she whispered. "No way she'll want to sing that way. You'll get your
song back."

It was the perfect plan! Zee imagined Kathi with her new "tan," and she had to stifle a laugh.

Slowly Chloe turned the knob up high. She was just about to push the spray button when Zee grabbed her arm to stop her. Then Zee turned the knob back to its low setting.

"Don't you want to beat her?" Chloe whispered.

"Of course!" Zee told her in her softest voice. "But I can't beat her if she doesn't compete. Besides, no matter how mean she is to me, I won't go down to her level."

"The best revenge," Chloe said, "will be when you get the *Teen Sing* recording contract."

High Note

Did you find what you were looking for?
Just ask me. I'm an open book.
Maybe it's you, telling yourself a lie,
About all you're feeling inside.
Give it a try! Open up that book.

Read me. Read me.
I'm an open book.
Read me. Read me.
Take more than just one look.

Thanks to Mr. P's inspiration, Zee had had no trouble writing a new song for *Teen Sing*. For a week, she had spent every moment that she wasn't studying or going to school—or hanging out with Chloe and Jasper—working on the lyrics. Mr. P was a big help. Now, she was in her room, smoothing out the words and getting the sound right.

Do you care that you took thoughts that were mine?
My eyes only. I'm an open book.

"Ohmylanta!" Zee stopped and slumped her body over the guitar across her lap. The melody just wasn't working. "I give up." She tossed the sheet music up in the air. It was too hard. She had made a mess of the first weeks of school, and she'd probably make a mess of this, too.

Knock. Knock. Zee looked at her door. She hadn't heard anyone come upstairs.

"Come in!" she shouted and started to put her guitar in its case.

Adam opened the door a bit. "Why'd you stop singing?"

"Because it's a stupid song," Zee said, waving a sheet of lyrics. "Who am I trying to kid? Kathi's the superstar—not me."

With giant steps, Adam strode across the room, took

the paper from Zee's hand, and picked up her guitar. "Move over," he commanded, then sat down on the bed.

Jerking his head to emphasize the beat, Adam played. *"'Did you find what you were looking for?'"* he sang. *"'Just ask me. I'm an open book.'"* The words sounded like an angry accusation—which was how Zee had felt when she'd written them. Only she hadn't ever actually sung them that way. Adam was rocking the song—and it sounded ten times better.

When Adam came to the end of the page, he stopped. Zee looked around the room for the next sheet. Her parents were standing in the doorway. How long had they been there?

"Who wrote that?" Mr. Carmichael asked Adam.

"Zee did," Adam said and handed her back the guitar.

"I thought your new song was about lipstick," Zee's father said.

Zee laughed. "Fingernail polish," she corrected. "Actually Mr. P helped me find a better subject."

Mrs. Carmichael's mouth dropped open. "Your music teacher helped you with *that*?" Zee nodded. "You're lucky to have someone who encourages you to express yourself so well."

"He sounds like a great teacher," Mr. Carmichael agreed.

"He is," Zee said. "But he might get fired. Some parents don't like the fact that he doesn't focus on classical music."

Zee's parents exchanged a concerned look. "Well, we'll leave you two to work on the song," Mr. Carmichael finally said. He clasped his wife's arm and guided her out of the room.

 SPARKLEGRRL: How's your song going?

 E-ZEE: Great. Mostly.

 SPARKLEGRRL: Mostly?

 E-ZEE: Every1 at school will know y I wrote it. Sometimes I'm afraid I say 2 much.

 SPARKLEGRRL: U? Saying too much? Nooooo.

 E-ZEE: LOL! Adam is going to play with me. He convinced me 2 change my style a little.

 SPARKLEGRRL: Just b tru 2 urslf and u'll b gr8. E-Zee 4 u, right?

TONIGHT'S THE Night !!

❋ ⑱ ❋

The Audition

Dear Diary,

I have NEVER been more nervous in my whole life!!! (And I probably won't ever be again until my first kiss with Landon. ☺) Today's the

Teen Sing

audition. For real. Really real. It's like the most important day EVER. Adam (or as I like to call him, "my band") and I have been practicing like crazy. He says I'm becoming a diva, but I just want it to be good. (And I kind of like the idea of being a diva!! Don't tell Adam.)

I had that dream again. No, not the bra one. This is the one where I'm up onstage with all the other Teen Sing contestants. My knees are shaking, and my hands are sweating. (Really gross sweating.) We're waiting for them to announce the winner.

The emcee—who else? Ryan Seacrest—opens the envelope, clears his throat, and turns to the contestants. "And the winner is—" That's when I wake up.

But I always think I hear my name just as I open my eyes. ☺

Zee

＊ ＊ ＊

Nobody at Brookdale Upper School got any work done the day of the audition—unless you call practicing their songs work, which Zee did. As she passed through the hall between classes, she sang her song. At lunch, she sang her song. And in gym, she made sure to get out quickly in dodgeball— no problem—so she could sing her song.

None of the teachers even bothered to lead a lesson— except Mr. P, who let Zee and Kathi perform for the class.

"You sounded great!" Chloe said, giving her a huge hug.

"It'll sound way better with Adam backing me up," Zee told her. Of course, the sound of Adam's name made Chloe blush.

Jasper remained as cool as ever through the entire day. Whenever Zee started to freak out, Jasper put down his book and reassured her. "You've got nothing to worry about. You'll be brilliant!"

After school in the locker room, Zee changed into the dress she had gotten from her dad's office and a pair of mid-calf boots in soft tan leather. She'd made a choker with a cloth strap and a delicate purple bead. Zee carefully positioned a cool knitted cap on her head. She'd found it at a flea market for a dollar. She looked in the mirror, pulling the sides of the hat down *just enough*, then at Chloe. "There! What do you think?"

"I think you look awesome!" Chloe stared at Zee.

"Then let's get to the auditorium before I chicken out!" She grabbed Chloe's arm and dragged her out of the locker room.

The girls didn't get far. A crush of people clogged the halls. "How am I going to find Adam in this mess?" Zee asked.

Chloe kicked into superhero mode. Practically dragging Zee behind her, she cleared a path in front of her so they could pass. "Coming through, y'all! Coming through!" she shouted. "This girl needs to get to the auditorium."

Through the windows, Zee could see men in bright orange vests directing traffic through the parking lot. "Ohmylanta! There's a TV crew outside!" she said to Chloe.

"Maybe they'll interview *you*!" Chloe said.

"Whenever I go to a movie premiere with my dad, I always wonder what it would be like to be one of the stars on the red carpet," Zee said dreamily. "Maybe this is my chance to find out!"

"That would be awesome!" Chloe said.

The auditorium was buzzing even more than the halls and parking lot. Zee searched the crowd—until a pair of waving arms caught her attention. Zee's mom was motioning to her from across the room. Next to her were her dad and Chloe's mom. And Adam. She had never been so happy to see her brother.

Everybody hugged Zee and wished her luck. Chloe gave

her the biggest hug of all. "Don't forget me when you're a famous singer, okay?" she said.

"I won't—if you promise not to forget me when you're a famous cellist," Zee answered.

"Hey, your *band* is ready," Adam said.

"Let's do it!" Zee exclaimed.

"I told you I'd let you wear a little makeup, Zee," Mrs. Carmichael said, opening her purse. "Do you want me to put it on you?"

"No, thanks," Zee said. "I'm going to be me tonight."

As Zee and Adam went to the contestants' waiting area, she scanned the crowd. Jasper was sitting in the middle of all the chaos, reading his book. Landon was right next to him. He had decided not to compete after all and had barely made eye contact with Zee since the day of the whiteboard message. But when he saw Zee, he elbowed Jasper, who looked up and smiled wide. Then Landon gave her a big thumbs-up!

Zee passed by the stage where Marcus was arranging some cables. He held his hand up for a high-five. Then he pointed at Zee and said, "I'll make sure you sound best." He paused, then added, "Oh, wait! You already do."

The only person missing was Ally. More than anyone else, Ally knew how important winning *Teen Sing* was to Zee. She knew how important *everything* was to Zee.

Zee was unpacking her guitar when she heard John Rock, a DJ from LA's most popular radio station, announce, "Ladies and gentlemen! Welcome to Brookdale Academy, home of the Los Angeles Region *Teen Sing* competition." The crowd erupted with screams and cheers. "In this room tonight are *the most talented* young voices in the area—and one of them will move on to the na-tion-al *Teen Sing* competition." Chills ran up and down Zee as the noise got louder. "Let's welcome our first *Teen Sing* contestant, Brookdale's very own Sam Bartholomew!"

Zee couldn't believe it. *Teen Sing* was really here. In Brookdale. At her school. And she was actually a contestant. By the end of the night, she could even be its winner!

Soon Zee's excitement switch turned off as John Rock announced, "Our next performer wrote this song by herself—and she's only a seventh grader. Kathi Barney."

Kathi's gorgeous voice floated through the auditorium. *"Jump into the water—it's cooler, baby."* Zee's words—and Kathi's lie. But she sounded fantastic. Zee's heart sank. Would she be able to outshine Kathi with her song from the heart?

Zee didn't have long to think about it. "Number twenty-four," a woman with a clipboard shouted.

"That's me!" Zee called out, waving her arms.

Clipboard Lady pointed at her. "You're in the hole."

"I don't know what that means," Zee said to Adam, worried.

"It's from baseball. It means there are two people ahead of you," he told her, laughing. "You know, it wouldn't hurt you to know *something* about sports."

"I'd rather speak English."

Adam put his hand on top of Zee's head and spun her so that she faced the door. "Let's go wait by the stage," he suggested.

When they reached the stage stairs, Adam pulled something out of the back pocket of his blue jeans. "I was going to wait to give this to you, but I'd rather do it now." He handed her a small book.

"A diary!" Zee flipped it over and ran her hands across the bumpy orange cloth cover.

"I didn't want you to have to keep using that homemade *math* binder."

"How'd you know that was my diary?" she asked.

"You never actually used it for math."

Zee hugged her brother while the next singer went onstage.

"You're after him, Twenty-four," Clipboard Lady said, pointing the eraser of her pencil at the top of the stairs. "You can go wait backstage."

Zee gulped and slowly ascended the steps with Adam close behind. Her legs felt like Jell-O.

As she waited at the top, Zee heard Clipboard Lady's nasal tone. "Contestants only, sir."

"But I need to give something to one of the performers," a frazzled voice responded. Mr. P!

"Sorry. You're too late."

Was Zee's teacher looking for her? She turned around and started to walk back down the stairs. "Hi, Mr. P."

"Let's give a *Teen Sing* welcome to Brookdale Academy seventh grader Mackenzie Blue Carmichael!" John Rock announced.

"We're up!" Adam called. Zee faced her brother.

"Wait!" Mr. P sounded frantic. Gripping the rail for support, he leaned and reached his arm up the stairs as far as he could. Zee reached down. Their fingertips met in the middle, and he handed off a small red triangle of plastic. A guitar pick? "Bob Dylan gave that to me in Berlin," Mr. P explained.

"Wow!"

"Come on," Adam urged.

"Thanks, Mr. P!" Zee said.

"Hmmm. Maybe Mackenzie Blue got cold feet," John Rock joked a few feet away. The audience laughed in confusion.

"Better hurry!" Clipboard Lady barked.

Zee turned to go onstage.

"Mackenzie!" Mr. P shouted. She stopped and turned. "Rock on!" he said with a smile.

"I guess we'll have to move on to the next contestant," the emcee said.

Zee smiled back at Mr. P. "I will!" she told him, then raced to the microphone. The bright lights shone down on her so that the audience was just a blur. Where were her parents? And Chloe? And Jasper? Her palms began to sweat. She wasn't sure she could play.

Then Zee remembered the pick in her hand. Bob Dylan was a legend—one of the best singer-songwriters. Ever. She wanted people to say that about her someday. She closed her eyes. The crowd dissolved. Ally's words came to Zee—"Just b tru 2 urslf"—and her fears vanished.

Zee lifted her right hand high over her head and played the first chord.

What do you see? It matters how you look.
It's just me. I'm an open book.
We're all scared, trying to hide,
Keeping secrets inside.

Not me! I've tried, but I'm an open book.
Read me. Read me.
I'm an open book.
Read me. Read me.
Take more than just one look.

Zee looked over at her brother. He gave her a nod that told her he was thinking exactly what she was thinking—they sounded better than they ever had.

With each verse, Zee grew more confident. She took some chances—changing her phrasing in some places, her style in others. Adam was right with her. He practically read her mind.

Zee was so into the song, she nearly forgot about all the eyes watching her. Then she did something she'd never done in rehearsal. After the song ended and the guitar strings stopped vibrating, after total silence filled the auditorium, she whispered, "I'm an open book," and hung her head.

Zee had no idea where the words came from. It was a complete improvisation. The crowd remained silent. Had she completely embarrassed herself? Did she sound like a freak? She looked up at the stunned audience, but she still couldn't see their faces.

Suddenly, the crowd in the seats went nuts—cheering, screaming, clapping, and whistling. Zee held her guitar high over her head, then took a big bow. And another. As she stumbled off the stage in a daze, kids crowded around her.

"That was great!" an eighth-grade boy said.

"You're an inspiration," one of the perfect-hair girls from the first day of school told her.

Chloe, Jasper, Marcus, and Landon found her. Of course, Kathi and Jen were nowhere around. *Phew!*

"You were amazing! Totally the best!" Chloe gushed.

"Good show!" Jasper said. "That was definitely worth putting my book down for!"

Landon punched Zee in the shoulder. "Awesome!" he said. Then he held up his phone and took her picture. "I'm going to show everyone when you get famous." It wasn't long before Mr. P and Zee's parents arrived with Chloe's mom. Mrs. Carmichael was clutching a tissue.

Mr. P looked at Zee. "It's nice to see a few friendly faces after you perform, isn't it?"

Zee could barely breathe, let alone answer her teacher. Her mother had her and Adam in a group hug that had somehow turned into a Zee squash. "My babies," Mrs. Carmichael said, finally releasing her children to breathe again.

At the end of the audition, John Rock tore open the envelope in his hand. "The winner . . . of the . . . Los Angeles Region *Teen Sing* . . . is . . . "

 E-ZEE: Guess what? I'm a star!

19

The Band

 SPARKLEGRRL: U WON!!!???

 E-ZEE: No, a jr named Carina Wyatt did.

 SPARKLEGRRL: I'm sorry.

 E-ZEE: It's OK. It would have been awesome
2 b the Teen Sing champion, but it was
definitely the best nite of my life.

 SPARKLEGRRL: Don't give up on ur
dream.

The next morning, Zee did a double-take as she walked into music class. She nearly didn't recognize the man at the front of the room. Mr. P looked like he'd gotten a great night's sleep for the first time since school had started. Actually it looked like he'd gotten an entire makeover. His hair was carefully groomed, the bags under his eyes had disappeared, and his button-down shirt was neatly tucked into his ironed dress pants.

"What's going on?" Zee asked suspiciously, walking sideways to her seat. She didn't take her eyes off Mr. P.

"Nothing," Mr. P answered. "Why?"

Zee decided it would be inappropriate to tell Mr. P that it looked like a secret government squad of spa technicians had reprogrammed him. "No reason."

Chloe was already there. She looked at Zee and shrugged, then said, "I still think you're way better than Carina."

"You even wrote your own song," Jasper added.

"Yeah, but Carina does have an incredible voice," Zee pointed out.

"By the time you're a junior, yours will be even better," Marcus said.

Zee smiled. "I hope so."

Brrrrng! At the sound of the first-period bell, Mr. P stepped to the front of his class. He took a deep breath. "I have big news for everyone." Big news? Zee thought about seeing him near Chloe's mom the night before. A knot tightened in Zee's stomach, and the worst thought bounced into her head. Was Mr. P about to say good-bye? Did he look better now because he was happy to be leaving?

What was Zee going to do without him? He was the one who had made her want to keep going when she was ready to give up. She blurted out, "Did you get fired?" Immediately, she slapped her hand across her mouth, afraid more words might escape if she didn't.

Mr. P laughed. "No," he said calmly. "This is good news. Actually, *great* news." Every student's eyes were locked on him. Even Kathi seemed interested in what he was about to say. "I was really impressed with the performances I saw last night. And I know that even those of you who didn't compete have a lot of musical talent."

The curious kids looked at one another. No one knew what Mr. P was going to say next. "A lot of people offered suggestions to make this class the best it can be," he continued. "I listened to their ideas, and they listened to mine. We collaborated to come up with a solution. And now I want you to collaborate." What was Mr. P trying to say? Zee wondered. "You're going to be a band."

"I thought we already were," Kathi said.

Mr. P nodded. "A different kind of band."

"Like a marching band?" Marcus asked. "Because it would be hard to march with a piano."

"And a cello," Chloe said, giggling.

"No, you're going to be a rock band. You'll play your instruments—and sing."

Kathi twisted up her face. "A *rock* band? But—"

Mr. P held up his hand and cut her off. "We'll also focus on the fundamentals of music—scales, études, whatever it takes. When I went to Juilliard—"

"You went to Juilliard?" Kathi cut him off this time. She was clearly impressed with Mr. P's credentials.

Everyone was. The class buzzed with excitement. Zee's musical career *really* was beginning.

 E-ZEE: This is better than winning Teen Sing.

 SPARKLEGRRL: Really?

 E-ZEE: I get 2 b in a band w Landon.

 SPARKLEGRRL: LOL. U can combine ur 2 fave things—singing & Landon.

 E-ZEE: C? Perfect. And the diary Adam gave me has a lock & key.

 SPARKLEGRRL: Do u think he made a copy of the key?

 E-ZEE: No. He can just read my mind instead of my diary. I'm an open book!

More than anyone, Ally already knew that. After all, even thousands of miles away, she still had Zee figured out.

Online Glossary

@	At
1	One
2	To; Too
2day	Today
2nite	Tonight
4	For
4get	Forget
8	Ate
ARFN	Au Revoir For Now
B	Be
BC	Because
B4	Before
BFF	Best Friend Forever
C	See
Every1	Everyone
E-zee	Easy

Fave	Favorite
G2G (or GTG)	Gotta Go
Gr8	Great
H8	Hate
HW	Homework
IDK	I Don't Know
K	Okay
LOL	Laugh Out Loud
LYLAS	Love You Like a Sister
M	Am
Mayb	Maybe
Nite	Night
OMG	Oh my God
Pls	Please
R	Are
Sez	Says
Tho	Though
Tru	True
U	You
Ur	Your; You Are
Urslf	Yourself
W	With
W8	Wait
Y	Why

Acknowledgments

First and foremost, I must thank Mackenzie's godmothers—Catherine Onder and Phoebe Yeh, who helped me breathe life into this series. Thank you for only giving me the best and making this book all it could be. Special thanks to the rest of my book team: Susan Katz, Elise Howard, Kate Jackson, Diane Naughton, Cristina Gilbert, Jim McKenzie, and Megan Howard. You've made this experience such a pleasure. And a special thank-you to Michael Segawa for bringing these characters to life.

To my A Team: Kate Lee, you are so much more than a fabulous agent. Thank you for believing in me and Mackenzie. Andre Des Rochers, thank you for being more than a great attorney. Thank you for speaking for me when I couldn't speak for myself at those most critical times! And to Melissa Breaux, my wonderful manager, thank you for organizing my mess of a life and making everything fall into place. And an honorable mention must be extended to the greatest quarterback of all quarterbacks, my dear friend Marissa Nance. Thanks for always pushing me when I needed it and introducing me to the people who made my dreams come true.

Mom and Dad, can you believe this? I want to say, who would've thought I'd end up here, but somehow I know you knew all along, and every day whispered words of encouragement to me, and offered prayers for me that I didn't even hear. I will never be able to thank you enough. Okay, one last note of thanks, for creating my best friends in the world: Adrianne, Erica, Marcus, Lisa, and William. You're the best friends and confidants a sister could ask for.

And finally, to the people who keep me sane: Michelle Moragne, Monica Rush, Nurys Iza, Suny Rodriguez, Jackie Fucini, Melissa Nasir, and Tina Pittaoulis—thanks for being the best friends a girl could ask for. Here's to more shopping trips and lots of laughs.

Curious to know what happens next
to Mackenzie and her friends?
Read on for a sneak peek at

Mackenzie Blue

The
Secret Crush

"Anyone else?" Mr. P—short for Mr. Papademetriou—looked at the seventh graders in his instrumental music class. He held a black dry-erase marker, ready to write on the whiteboard at the front of the classroom. The students sat silent. "Come on. We're brainstorming names for our band. There's no such thing as a bad idea."

Landon Beck flicked his head to move the sun-bleached bangs that hung slightly over his eyes. "How about Seven Up?" he suggested. "You know, 'cause there are seven members of the group."

That's an amazing idea! Mackenzie Blue Carmichael thought. Of course, Landon was so cute, everything he said sounded great.

"Good one!" Kathi Barney cheered from the seat in front of Zee. Kathi's positive reaction didn't surprise Zee. She and Landon used to be a couple in sixth grade. Most of the time, Kathi acted like they still were.

"Seventh-Grade Singers?" Jen Calverez, Kathi's best friend, chimed in.

"The Brookdale Best!" Marcus Montgomery said.

Mr. P wrote quickly, putting each suggestion on his list under the ones that were already there—the Firecrackers, Cinnamon Toast, and Time Zone.

Zee adjusted the clips that she'd put into her red bob that morning. She had decorated them with tiny pink and purple plastic rhinestones from the craft shop. "How about the Zippers?" Zee suggested.

Kathi groaned as Mr. P wrote Zee's band name suggestion on the board. "Why? So it can be like Zee and the Zippers?" she asked. "No way!"

Zee shrugged. "I just think it sounds cool."

"It's brilliant!" Jasper Chapman defended Zee. Jasper had moved to Brookdale from London over the summer, and he was one of Zee's best friends.

"Thanks," Zee mouthed, giving Jasper a thumbs-up. He smiled.

"Keep 'em coming. There are some really cool ideas here, guys," Mr. P said.

"Total Eclipse!" Zee's other best friend, Chloe Lawrence-Johnson, another Brookdale newbie, called out in her Southern accent.

Slumping forward a little, Kathi let out a bored sigh. Chloe turned to her and stared with expectant eyes. "Everything all right, Kathi?"

Kathi just flicked her shiny long brown hair off her shoulder. "Of course," she said, without turning around.

"Zodiac!" Landon added.

Yay! Zee silently cheered.

But there was another groan, and this time it came from the seat beside Zee. *Jasper?* Zee silently wondered. *What's up with that?* Jasper turned and gave her another smile.

"How about The Beans?" Kathi suggested.

"That's awesome!" Jen said. Usually, she said *everything* Kathi did was awesome—just to make her happy. But this time Zee agreed. The whole class started buzzing.

"Should we vote?" Mr. P broke in. "Who likes The Beans?"

Everyone's hand went up.

"It's unanimous!" Mr. P said as he erased the list on the board. "You are officially The Beans." The class cheered.